# THE W. HEATH ROBINSON Illustrated STORY BOOK

A magic harp helps a poor young man to win the hand of a beautiful princess; a band of monkeys rescue a prince from attack by a giant serpent; a boy's kindness to an old lady is rewarded with a king's crown – in the world of fairy-tale all kinds of strange and wonderful things can happen. This collection of thirteen stories contains all the well-known and loved ingredients of fairy-tale and is beautifully illustrated by W. Heath Robinson.

W. Heath Robinson was born in 1872 and died in 1944. Together with his two brothers, he illustrated work by Hans Andersen, Edgar Allen Poe, Kipling, Perrault and Walter de la Mare, to name but a few. He also contributed humorous drawings to several English and American magazines and designed comic scenery for theatre productions.

# THE
# W. HEATH ROBINSON
## Illustrated
# STORY BOOK

W. HEATH ROBINSON

BEAVER
BOOKS

First published in 1979 by
The Hamlyn Publishing Group Limited
London · New York · Sydney · Toronto
Astronaut House, Feltham, Middlesex, England

ISBN 0 600 20015 9

Printed in England by
G. A. Pindar & Son Limited, Scarborough
Set in Monophoto Bembo

The stories in this collection were originally published in
*Playbox Annual* from 1916 to 1921 and are the copyright of
IPC Magazines Limited. The publishers are grateful to the
latter for permission to reproduce this material.

# CONTENTS

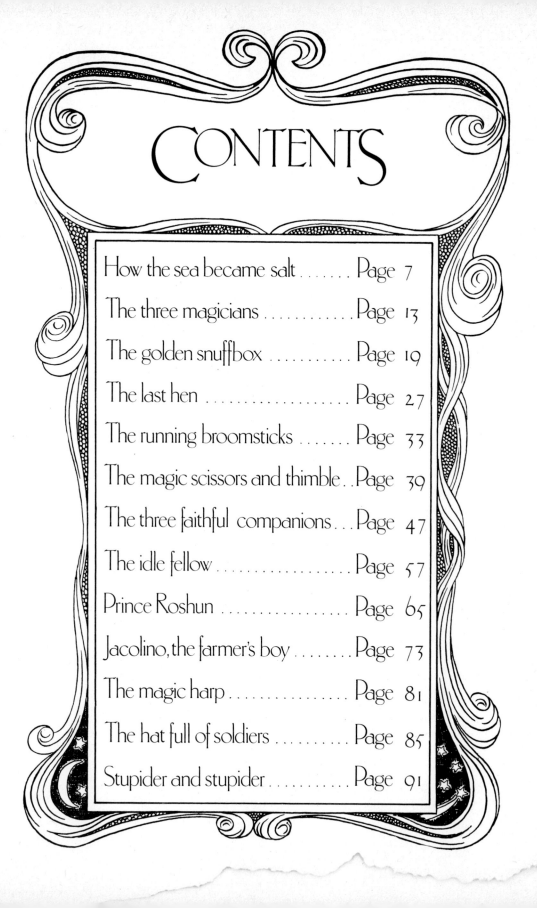

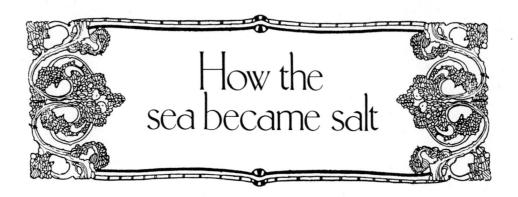

# How the sea became salt

ONCE upon a time there were two brothers, one of whom was rich, the other poor. One Christmas Eve the poor man, who had not a crumb of bread to eat, went to his brother and begged him to give him something.

His brother was anything but pleased to see him, and so, while the poor fellow was still some distance off, the rich man called out to him:

'If you will promise to do as I say, I will give you one of those big hams which are hanging in the chimney.

'Here is the ham. Now, *go away*, and never come begging here again!'

The poor brother went away, carrying his ham. He walked all day long, and in the evening, just as it was growing dark, he met an old man who had a long white beard.

'Good evening!' said the poor wanderer.

'Good evening!' said the man with the beard. 'And where may you be going?'

'I am going home to my wife.'

'First go a little farther,' said the old man, 'and you will come to an enchanter's castle. As soon as you enter it, his imps will crowd around you, wishing to buy that ham which you are carrying on your shoulder, because among enchanters' imps ham is a rare treat. But be sure you *do not sell it for money*. Ask, in exchange, for an old coffee-grinder which you will see by the door. When you have got it,

come back to me, and I will show you what to do with it.'

The traveller thanked the old man for his advice, then went on to the castle. He knocked

at the door, and was invited in. Inside, every-thing was just as he had been told it would be. The imps gathered round him and wanted him to give them the ham.

'I had intended,' said the man, 'to eat it at home with my wife this Christmas Eve; but since you have taken such a fancy to it, I will give it to you, and ask nothing in exchange but that old coffee-grinder by the door.'

The imps at first objected to part with the grinder. They began to argue and bargain, but the man would take nothing else; and so at last he went off with the old thing.

He found the long-bearded man again, who showed him how to use the grinder. To set it going, he had merely to tell it what he wished for; but to make it stop grinding, he had to place it in a certain position.

After thanking his kind friend, the poor man turned towards his home, and, though he hurried as fast as he could, it was pitch-dark by the time he arrived there.

'Where have you been all this time?' inquired his wife. 'I have been waiting for you hour after hour, and I have not as much as a grain of flour with which to make you a Christmas cake.'

'I could not come earlier,' replied the man, 'for I have had to walk a long, long way. But see what I have brought you!'

He put the coffee-grinder on the table, wished for supper, and turned the handle. At once the table was covered with a cloth, lights, food and drink. It was a splendid Christmas feast. Whatever the coffee-grinder was told to do, it did immediately.

The woman looked on in amazement. Presently she asked where the grinder came from, but her husband refused to answer this question.

'Do not trouble your head about that,' he said. 'Be content to enjoy the good things it provides.'

So they began to eat and drink.

On the third day after Christmas they gave a grand dinner-party, to which they invited all their friends. The rich brother, who was present, was so excited that beads of perspiration stood out on his forehead.

'Tell me how it is,' he said, 'that, though on Christmas Eve you were so poor and came begging for bread, you are now entertaining as if you were a king or a duke. Where on earth does this sudden wealth come from?'

'I found it behind a door,' replied his brother, who did not intend to part with his secret.

On another night, however, he could keep it to himself no longer and told his brother the story of the coffee-grinder.

From that time on the rich man set his heart on possessing this marvellous thing. At last his brother agreed to sell it to him for three hundred pounds, on condition that he should keep it in his own possession until harvest-time.

'By then,' said the 'poor' brother to himself,

'I can get enough treasure out of the coffee-grinder to last me for years.'

And so you will understand that he made the most of his time, and did not let the coffee-grinder rust for want of use. Then, when harvest-time came round, he gave it up; but he did not tell his brother how to *stop* it, and his brother, I suppose, did not think of asking.

It was night when the rich man took the coffee-grinder to his house. The next day he told his wife to go to the fields with the reapers, while he stayed at home and prepared the midday meal.

At dinner-time, he put the coffee-grinder on the table, and gave an order.

'Serve us with herrings and milk-soup,' he commanded.

Then the coffee-grinder began to fill all the dishes, all the pots, all the kitchen with herrings and soup. The man turned it first one way, then another. In vain! The coffee-grinder would *not* stop! Soon the flood of soup had risen to such a height that the man was in danger of drowning. He opened the door of the room; the passages were quickly filled.

When, with difficulty, he managed to reach and open the hall-door, the torrent of milk-soup, with its floating herrings, dashed out into the garden.

Meanwhile, his wife, at work in the fields, was getting hungry, and wondering why her husband did not call her in to dinner.

'Let us go back to the house,' she said to the reapers. 'My husband must have been unable to get the dinner ready. I will go and help him.'

They went towards the house, and were met by a stream of milk-soup and herrings. Through this ever-rising flood waded the rich brother.

'I wish,' he exclaimed, 'that each one of you had a hundred throats! Take care that this dinner does not drown you!'

Then he ran as fast as he could to his brother's house, begging and praying him to take back his coffee-grinder.

'If it goes on like this for only an hour,' said the rich brother, 'the entire village will be submerged, and disappear under the milk-soup and herrings!'

The 'poor' brother agreed to take back the coffee-grinder, but he charged three hundred pounds for doing so. The rich brother was at his mercy; the only thing he could do was to pay the money at once, and so stop that dreadful coffee-grinder.

With this money, and some more provided by the coffee-grinder, the once poor brother built for himself a splendid house. Its walls were covered with gold, and, as it stood close to the sea, its glittering front was reflected in the water. The house could be seen from far away, and the fame of its lucky owner spread abroad. Many people came – some from long distances – to visit him.

Amongst these was the captain of a passing ship, who wanted to see the coffee-grinder. He asked whether it could produce salt, and, when told that it *could* do so, he resolved to buy it, no matter at what price.

'For when I have this coffee-grinder,' he thought, 'I shall no longer have to voyage over the sea in order to obain cargoes of salt. I shall become rich without taking any trouble, just by selling the salt from the coffee-grinder.'

And when the captain had been begging a long time for the coffee-grinder, the once poor (but now rich) man agreed to sell it for a huge sum.

As soon as the captain had it, he hurried away (for fear that the seller might want it back again) without taking the trouble to ask any questions about the proper use of the coffee-grinder. He took it on board his ship, and, when she was right out at sea, he stood it on the deck, and said to it:

'Bring me salt.'

And it brought him salt. The ship was filled with salt. The captain then tried to stop the working of the coffee-grinder, but, whichever way he turned it, it went on pouring out salt.

The ship broke down with the weight and quickly sank. The coffee-grinder fell to the bottom of the sea, where it is still ceaselessly grinding out salt.

And this is the reason that the sea is salt.

# The three magicians

ONCE upon a time there were seven little princes and princesses whose father was a brave king who fought hard to rid his country of giants, witches, dragons and other strange monsters who troubled it in those days. Their father often rode out to the wars, but the seven little princes and princesses lived at home in the palace, and made themselves merry all the day.

One day they were out in the palace garden playing 'I spy' among the rose bushes, when they saw three strange old men all walking together, leaning on staffs, smiling at them through the railings of the castle.

The little princes and princesses had never seen such quaint-looking old men before, so they all stopped their game to crowd up to the railings, and asked them who they were.

'Oh, we are three magicians from the East!' said the three old men. 'What dear little children you are, to be sure! How much we should like to come in and show you some conjuring tricks.'

'And so you shall!' said the eldest little princess, whose name was Isa. 'There is a little wicket-gate near here, and I will go to the porter and ask him to let you in!'

So the little princess ran off to the wicket-gate to call the porter to let the three old magicians in. But the porter was not there, for the truth was the magicians had given him a piece of silver money to go away and leave the key in the gate.

The Princess Isa and all the other little princes and princesses were quite anxious to see the three old men do conjuring tricks, so they never thought of going to the palace to ask for leave, but just opened the gate and let the magicians into the rose garden.

The three magicians showed the children several amusing tricks, and they were all charmed by them, for there was not one which could frighten them in the least.

Presently one of the magicians took a queer little glass box out of his pocket, held it up before the princes and princesses, and said:

'Would you like to have a look into this?'

The little princes and princesses each had a look, and there they saw a little man no bigger than your thumb running about inside the box.

He was wonderfully dressed, in robes like a king, and they could hear his voice shouting faintly: 'Let me out! Let me out!' from inside the glass box.

'Shall I let him out?' said the magician, grinning at the little princes and princesses.

'Oh, yes! Poor little man!' they shouted. 'Why should he be shut up in that glass box?'

'Take care what you say,' said the magician. 'For if I let him out he will grow large, and I shall not be able to put him back again.'

'Oh, never mind!' said the Princess Isa. 'Let

him out and he can grow as big as he likes!'

So the magician opened the box, and let out the tiny man who was dressed like a little emperor.

The moment he did so the little man began to swell and grow, so that the eye could hardly follow his growth. In a minute he was over a foot high. In two minutes he was two feet high, in three he was as large as one of the children.

But he did not stop there; he went on swelling and growing until he became a great full-blown giant, wearing the robes of an emperor, and then he stopped. And all the time he was growing the three magicians laughed and laughed till the tears poured down their cheeks.

And the little princes and princesses laughed too, for they did not realise what danger they were running into.

But the Giant did not laugh. He looked very proud and haughty.

And when he had finished growing, he stamped his foot upon the ground, and cried out:

'I am the Emperor of the Giants, and all this country is no longer the King's, but mine!'

And then the little princes and princesses stopped laughing, especially when the Giant turned to them and said: 'Who are you?'

'We are the little princes and princesses,' said the little Princess Isa. 'And this country does not belong to you, but to our father, the King!'

'We'll see about that!' said the Giant, and he picked up the little princes and princesses and stuffed them all into his pocket.

'Now!' said the Giant to the three magicians. 'You are my counsellors and advisers. Tell me what to do next! For though I am a great Giant, and the Emperor of all the Giants, I know very well I cannot fight against all the people in this country unless I have a safe place to hide in!'

'We know that!' said the three magicians. 'But not very far from here there is a great castle standing on top of a high rock, which

men can only climb up to one at a time. You must go there at once, and take the little princes and princesses with you.

'This will make their father give up making war against the Giants and the Wizards, and you will be able to rule the country!'

So the Giant marched off with the little princes and princesses, and the people were so surprised that they could not prevent him.

The Giant went to the castle on the high rock, and there he kept the little princes and princesses with him. He did not attempt to hurt them, but let the people from the countryside come and look at them from far below.

'And now,' roared the Giant to the people, 'if you do not let me have any food to eat, they shall have none either!'

So the people were very frightened and troubled on account of the King, their master, of whom they were very fond, and who was now away in a far country at the wars.

So they sent all manner of food to the castle, and the Giant himself ate more than twenty sheep and oxen a day. And the more he ate the larger and stouter he grew; and because he got no exercise, his temper got worse every day of the week.

He made the three magicians cook for him, and they were soon sorry that they had to obey this new master.

For the Giant stormed and shouted at them all day, and when his dinner was late, or if it was not cooked to his liking, he threw the plates at them.

And very soon the three magicians told each other they had been silly old men to encourage such a monster as that, who never gave them any rest from cooking and washing-up, so that their lives became a burden to them and they had hardly time to cook a meal for themselves.

Meantime, the Princess Isa was worrying and thinking how she could free her little brothers and sisters. So she went hunting about the castle looking for a way out.

But the castle stood on top of a precipice, and

it would have needed a rope more than three hundred feet long to get her down safely.

One day she was passing by the kitchen where the three magicians were busy cooking, and she heard one of them say to the other:

'I am getting very tired of our friend the Giant, and I think we have earned our reward.

'Besides, I have heard that the King of this country is already marching with a large army to the relief of his children, and it is my belief this greedy man has grown so fat that he will not be able to strike a blow on his own behalf.'

'That's true!' said the second magician. 'It is a good thing we have the feathers in our pack ready to fit to our shoulders, so that we can fly back to China!'

'Tonight we will do it!' said the third magician. 'All we need do is to cry 'Hey,

Presto! Abracadabra!' and then we will fly away where we please, and leave the greedy monster to his fate!'

The little princess had no sooner heard this than she hurried off to the magicians' lodging, and searched hurriedly through their bundles, in great fear and trembling lest she should be found out.

She had not looked very long before she came on a bundle of strange feathers in one of

'The prisoners are escaping! We are lost!' cried the three magicians.

And they rushed to the very edge of the precipice and looked over.

them, and as soon as she had done so she hurried off at once to her little brothers and sisters. In the shoulder of each child she fastened two feathers, and last of all in her own.

'Now come to the castle wall, children! We are going to fly!' she cried.

So they all hurried off, and there was a great burst of cheering as they reached the castle wall.

For there below them was a long line of soldiers, with the King, their father, riding at the head, come to their rescue.

'What's the matter? What's the matter?' cried the three magicians, hurrying out, and just then, at the sight of them, the little Princess Isa cried out: 'Hey, Presto! Abracadabra!'

And at once all the feathers fluttered in the air, carrying the children off their feet and bearing them down safely to the foot of the castle rock.

Yes, the seven little princes and princesses had reached the ground quite safely, and the King, their father, was hugging first one and then the other, he was so delighted to see them again.

The soldiers, too, were cheering and waving their helmets with joy, for everyone loved the little princes and princesses.

'Oh, they've gone! They've escaped!' wailed the unhappy magicians again, wringing their hands. 'Oh, what shall we do? What shall we do?'

'What's that? What's that?' cried the Giant, dashing out of the door in pursuit; and the next moment he was rolling over and over to the foot of the precipice, where he suddenly disappeared. No one knew where he went, because no one saw him go. But anyway, he vanished right away.

The three magicians rushed to their bundles for the magic feathers with which to fly away, but not finding them, in their despair they changed themselves into three mice, and were never seen afterwards.

# The golden snuffbox

A LONG time ago, in an age so happy that neither you nor I will ever see its like, there lived an old man and an old woman. They had one son, who lived with them in the heart of a great forest. The boy had never seen anyone except his father and mother, but he read a great deal, and thus learnt that other people existed. In his books he found so many references to wonderful princesses that at last he decided that he simply must see one for himself.

One day, when his father had gone into the forest, the young man told his mother that he wished to leave her.

'I see nothing here,' he said, 'but great trees all round me, and if I stay here I shall never learn anything.'

The young man left his mother in tears, and presently met his father. The latter asked where he was going, and he repeated what he had already said to his mother.

'Very good, my son,' said the old man, embracing him. 'I am sorry to see you leave us, but since it is your own idea, it is best that you should go.'

A moment later, as Jack was setting off again, his father called him back, and took a golden snuffbox from his pocket.

'Take this little snuffbox,' he said. 'Hide it in your pocket, and open it only when you are in danger of death.'

The young man journeyed on for a long time, stopping only when he was exhausted. Night fell at last, and he could hardly see the road in front of him. In the distance a tiny light glimmered, and, directing his steps towards it, he reached a door, at which he knocked. A servant came to open it, and asked him what he wanted. Jack replied that he was looking for a night's lodging and supper. The servant gave him a meal, and while he was eating the young daughter of the house had the curiosity to come in and look at the stranger. His appearance must have pleased her greatly, for she went to her father and told him there was a charming young man in the kitchen.

Her father, in turn, was curious to make the latter's acquaintance. He questioned Jack as to what he was able to do, and the boy replied that he knew how to do everything.

'In that case,' said his host, 'see to it that at eight o'clock tomorrow morning there shall be an ocean in front of my house, and on the ocean some great ships. The biggest of the ships shall fire a gun in the king's honour, and the last bullet shall split in two the foot of the bed in which my daughter sleeps. If you do not carry out the whole of this task, you are a dead man!'

'Very good,' said Jack; 'there will be no difficulty about that.' And with these words, he went upstairs to his room, said his prayers, and fell asleep.

He awoke a little before eight o'clock, with barely time to remember his host's commands.

Then he remembered the snuffbox which his father had given him.

'Never,' he remarked to himself, 'have I been so near death as at this moment!'

He felt in his pockets, took out the golden snuffbox, and opened it. Out of it sprang three little red dwarfs, who exclaimed: 'What do you want from us?'

'I wish,' said Jack, 'that there should be at this very moment before this house an ocean, and on this ocean some great ships, the largest of which shall fire a gun in honour of the king, and the last bullet must split in two the foot of the bed on which my host's daughter is sleeping.'

'It will be done,' said the dwarfs. 'Sleep again.'

Before Jack could say another word, eight o'clock struck, and the report of a gun resounded through the air. He leaped out of bed, and I can assure you that no one was more astonished than he to find himself so well obeyed. He dressed, went downstairs, and met the master of the house.

'That was not at all badly done, young fellow,' said the latter, as he came up. 'You are certainly clever. Two more tasks, and I give you my daughter. But, first of all, to breakfast!'

Jack ate with an excellent appetite, and exchanged tender glances with the young girl.

The second task consisted of transporting all the trees in the garden a league away before the following morning, and, not to make our story too long, it will be enough to say that Jack succeeded, and his host was very pleased.

'There now remains only the third task,' said his host. 'You must build me a great castle resting on twelve golden pillars. In front of this castle I wish to see a regiment at drill, and at the moment when eight o'clock is striking the colonel must cry "Shoulder arms!"'

'I quite understand,' said Jack.

The next morning everything went as it should, and the young man received his host's daughter in marriage.

But Jack was not at the end of his troubles. There came a day when his father-in-law, who was a wealthy nobleman, arranged a great hunting party, to which he invited all his friends and neighbours, with the object of showing them the new mansion which Jack had built. Jack himself was told to assemble the guests in the hunting field and bring them all back to the castle, and his father-in-law presented him with a fine horse and a purple jacket. He put the jacket on and went off.

But during Jack's absence a servant felt in the pockets of his old coat and pulled out the golden snuffbox, which had been left behind. He opened it, and at once three red dwarfs came out and asked his wishes.

'I wish,' said the servant, 'that this castle shall be transported far from here to the other side of the ocean.'

'Good. Do you wish to be taken with it?'

'Yes.'

'Then climb up on the roof.'

The servant obeyed, and the castle took flight to the farther side of the ocean.

When the huntsmen returned there was no sign of the castle and not a trace of golden pillars! Everything had vanished, to the great disappointment of the guests.

The blame was laid on Jack, and his father-in-law gave him a year and a day in which to recover the lost castle. If he were not successful when this period of grace was up, his wife was to be taken from him. So the poor lad set forth, taking with him a good horse and a large sum of money.

He travelled up hill and down dale, through dark forests and over great deserts, and arrived one day at the palace of the King of the Mice. A small mouse was on guard before the door, and cried out: 'Halt! Who goes there?'

'I wish to see the king,' said the young man.

The king received him well, and asked him where he was going. Jack replied that he had lost a great castle, and was obliged to find it and bring it back to his father-in-law within a year and a day.

'We will look for it tomorrow,' said the king. 'For the moment, to dinner!'

Jack ate with excellent appetite, and slept soundly.

The next morning he accompanied the king to the parade ground, where all the mice in the world had been gathered by Royal order. A herald asked them if they knew of a great castle built on twelve pillars of gold.

'No!' they replied with one voice.

The King advised Jack to pay visits to his two elder brothers, the King of the Frogs and the King of the Birds.

'Seek them out,' he said, 'for possibly they will have heard tell of your palace. Here is a cake which you will deliver to the King of the Frogs, and by this token he will know that you have been sent to him by me. Do not forget to tell him that I am in good health, and that I shall be happy to have news of him.'

Jack took his leave, and just as he was crossing the threshold he noticed a little mouse, who begged him to take her with him. Fearing that to do so would displease the king, he refused, but the mouse insisted.

'Perhaps I shall be able to help you,' she said.

'Very well. Up with you.'

The mouse climbed all the way up the horse's leg, and so reached the young man's boot. He then picked her up and put her in his right-hand pocket.

After travelling a long way on the road, Jack at last reached the kingdom of the frogs. In front of the palace was a frog doing sentry duty, with a little gun on his shoulder, who cried out: 'Halt! Who goes there?'

'I wish to see the king,' said the young man; and he was admitted at once.

The king came to meet him, and Jack told his story again, right from the beginning to the end. When it was finished, they had supper and went to bed.

The next morning a shrill whistle pierced the air, and from all sides the frogs of all the world were seen hurrying up. The king asked if any of them was aware of a castle of twelve golden pillars, but none had seen it. So Jack left for the King of the Birds.

Just as he was leaving the palace, a small frog begged him to take her with him. He refused at first, but presently allowed himself to be persuaded, and put the little creature in his left-hand pocket.

He rode three times as far as on his previous journeys, and arrived at last at the palace of the eldest of the three brothers.

A charming little bird was mounting guard, but allowed the traveller to pass freely into the king's presence, where his tale was told once more.

W
HEATH
ROBINSON

'Very good,' said the king. 'Tomorrow I will summon my subjects, and they will tell you if they know your castle.'

Jack put his horse in the stable, had dinner, and went to bed.

The next morning the king took him into the fields and began to whistle. At once the birds of all the world flocked round them, but to the question which was put to them they replied that not one of them had seen the castle.

'Wait a moment,' said the king. 'I do not see here the greatest of you all.'

They waited for a little while, and then two little birds flew forth to look for the missing bird.

Soon an enormous eagle appeared, who seemed quite exhausted. The king asked him if he knew of a castle with twelve golden pillars.

'Yes,' said the eagle. 'I have just come from there.'

'That is good,' said the king. 'This young man has lost it. You will take him there as soon as you have had some rest and refreshment.'

A calf was killed, and the largest piece of it was given to the eagle, in order that he might gain strength for so long a journey. Then Jack climbed on the bird's back, and they flew off.

In due course they reached the famous castle, but were at a loss to know how to get back the golden snuffbox.

'Put me down on the ground,' said the little mouse whom the young man had brought. 'I shall have no difficulty in bringing it to you.'

She scurried into the castle and, after routing about in every corner, at length discovered the snuffbox, which she took to Jack. He placed it joyfully in his pocket, but did not open it. Before the castle was transported, he wanted to thank the King of the Birds. Then he climbed again on to the great eagle's back.

As the little band was crossing the ocean, a

quarrel broke out amongst the animals as to whether the eagle or the mouse had done the most for Jack. In the course of the quarrel, a sudden jerk caused the snuffbox to fall into the water.

'There!' said the frog. 'I knew quite well that you would need me.'

She plunged into the depths of the ocean, and was lost to sight for three days and nights. At the end of that time she pushed her nose out of the sea, in order to take breath. The rest flew down towards her, asking if she had found the snuffbox.

'No,' she said.

'Then what are you doing on the surface?'

'Nothing at all, but I must take breath.'

A moment later she dived again, and after searching for another day and night she at last brought back the precious object.

Continuing their journey, the travellers arrived, some four days later, at the home of the King of the Birds. The latter was overjoyed to see them, received them courteously, and talked to them for a long time.

At last Jack opened the snuffbox, and commanded the red dwarfs to find the castle. The dwarfs departed, and, despite their fears that the people in possession of the mansion might be at home, the latter proved, luckily, to be out. Only a kitchen-maid and a serving-girl were on the premises, and these were made to climb on to the roof.

Hardly had they got there when their masters returned. But the latter were too late — they could only raise their arms to the sky, and despairingly watch their castle flying at full speed through the air.

After a journey of nine days the spot was reached where the king and Jack were waiting. The king greatly admired the castle, and wished to climb the golden steps in order to inspect the inside. But the year and a day of grace was nearly at an end, and Jack, being anxious to see his young wife again, ordered the dwarfs to set him on his way.

When the journey was ended there was Jack's wife, coming to meet her husband with a chubby baby boy in her arms!

The young couple made their home in the castle, and lived there happily for a long time with the mouse and the frog.

# The last hen

ONCE a poor sexton lived in a village. It was with difficulty that he earned a living, but his wife kept a number of hens, and by selling the eggs in a neighbouring town they managed to keep body and soul together. But one day a dreadful misfortune befell them. The hens began to die quickly one after another, till at last there remained only one, which they were obliged to sell.

On the next market day, therefore, the sexton's wife set out for the town. On her back she carried a basket, in which she had placed the precious hen, and as the road lay over a mountain she was obliged to sit down occasionally in order to rest herself. While she was sitting a dwarf, whose long white beard fell almost to the ground, suddenly appeared before her.

'Where are you going?' asked the strange little man.

The poor woman was very scared, but managed to stammer out a reply.

'I am going to market,' she said, 'to sell my last hen.'

'Give me your hen,' said the dwarf, 'and I will give you a pot in return for it.'

The bargain seemed such a poor one that the woman forgot her fright and burst out laughing.

'That would be a poor exchange,' she said. 'My hen is far more valuable.'

'Do not be so sure,' replied the dwarf, 'that your hen is worth more than my pot. But if the bargain does not please you, I will not force you to it.'

The woman began to wonder whether the offer, after all, might not be a fair one, and after some consideration she agreed to accept. The dwarf at once vanished, but in a few moments returned with a black and rusty pot in his hand.

'So long as you have this pot,' he said, 'you will never be in need. You have only to place it in the shade, cover it, and say, "Pot, fill thyself!" and the pot will obey you. But be careful never to clean it, and do not let the sun shine on it.'

The woman promised to follow these instructions, took the pot, and went home. Naturally she was anxious to find out if her new possession really had the magic properties which the dwarf had described, and at the first opportunity she placed it in the shade and covered it with a cloth. Then she cried:

'Pot, fill thyself with milk!'

When the cloth was removed, the pot was full to the brim with milk! Overjoyed, she ran to her husband and told him of the good fortune that had come to them.

For a long time the pot remained in use, and never failed to give good service. But the more it was used, the blacker it became, and the woman, like a good housewife, itched to clean it. One day she noticed that it had become

blacker than ever, and, forgetting the dwarf's instructions, she set to and began to clean it. She rubbed and polished and polished and rubbed until the black had all been removed, and when she set the pot down in the sun it shone like pure gold. The sight delighted her, but when she stretched out her hand to pick the splendid object up, she received so violent a blow that she fell down in a swoon. When she came to herself the pot had vanished.

The loss of the precious pot was a disaster, for instead of plenty there was now want. Things went from bad to worse, till at last the wife told her husband that he had better go to the town in the hope that on the way he might fall in with the friendly dwarf.

So that he would not have to go empty-handed, the sexton borrowed some money and bought a lamb, which he took with him to the town. When he arrived at the spot on the mountainside where his wife had had the strange meeting, he sat down to rest. He waited for a long time but no one came. As he got up to continue his journey, however, he heard a movement in the bushes beside the road, and on turning his head he saw the little man with the long white beard standing beside him.

'Where are you going?' asked the dwarf.

The sexton began to tremble, finding his hopes so suddenly realised.

'I am driving this lamb to the market,' he said.

'Your trouble is for nothing,' said the dwarf. 'Among all the sheep with which the market is crowded, who will notice your one small lamb? Give it to me, and I will give you a ball in exchange.'

'Of what use is that to me?' said the sexton.

'With the money I get for my lamb I can buy as many balls as I want.'

Don't be so sure,' replied the dwarf, 'that you can get a ball like mine. But if you don't want to make the exchange, I won't take your lamb.'

At this point the sexton, remembering the pot, agreed to the bargain, and the dwarf went away. When he returned he brought with him a ball which seemed to be made of wood.

'When you want to use this ball,' said the dwarf, 'lay it on the ground, and say, "Ball, doff thy cap!" But on no account leave any door or window open when you do this.'

The sexton took the ball, but found it was so heavy that he could scarcely hold it. Slinging it in a handkerchief, he hurried home, eager to try it out. When he got home, he closed all windows and doors, laid the ball on the ground, and cried: 'Ball, doff thy cap!'

At once the ball began to move, rolling to and fro about the floor with ever-increasing speed. Faster and faster it travelled, until suddenly it split in two, and from each half there leapt out a number of little men, carrying golden dishes containing good food. These they put on the table, and at once vanished into the ball again.

With great delight the sexton and his wife sat down to such a meal as they had not enjoyed since the loss of the magic pot.

No sooner had they finished than the ball again divided and the same little company of dwarfs emerged. They removed all the dishes from the table, and carried them into the ball, which closed of its own accord as soon as the last had entered.

For a long time the sexton and his wife remained in possession of the ball, for, needless to say, they were careful not to repeat the mistake of disobeying the instructions they had received with it. But gradually news leaked out in the village of what a wonderful treasure the happy pair possessed, and the tale came to the ears of the abbot of the monastery. The latter sent at once for the sexton, and inquired if the story was true. The sexton was unwilling to admit it, but, under threat of losing his job, he confessed the whole story. In obedience to the abbot's orders he brought the ball to the monastery, where he was obliged to leave it, being promised in return a better job.

But the poor sexton waited so long without receiving the promised reward that he determined to try his luck once more in the mountains. He therefore bought two oxen, and drove them before him along the road to the town. Once more he rested at the same spot, and this time he had hardly sat down when the dwarf stood before him.

'Well, have you come for another ball?' asked the little man.

'Yes,' said the sexton; 'and as I wish for a better ball this time, I have brought two oxen.'

'Wait a moment,' said the dwarf, and vanished.

In due course he reappeared, carrying a larger ball than the former one. This he gave to the sexton, saying:

'You know what you have to do!'

Gratified by his success, the sexton went back home and started to try out the larger ball. He closed the doors and windows, placed it on the ground, and cried, 'Ball, doff thy cap!' Like its predecessor, the ball began to roll about, moving even faster than the small one. At last it divided just as before, but instead of a troop of dwarfs there came out two giants armed with huge cudgels, who swung them about so vigorously that before long the sexton lay swooning on the ground. Only then did the giants re-enter the ball.

The sexton now saw a way to get his revenge on the cheating abbot. He presented himself at the monastery with the new ball, and asked for an audience with the abbot. This was refused, because the abbot was entertaining a large party of guests. The sexton persisted in his request, however, and sent in word that he had now a much larger and better ball to display. This cunning message had the desired effect, for without more ado he was ushered into the great hall, where the abbot and his guests were dining.

The sexton was told to show what the ball could do for the amusement of the company. He set his burden down, and cried, 'Ball, doff thy cap!'

At once the ball split open, and before the unhappy guests could defend themselves the two giants emerged and laid about them with their clubs, not stopping until everybody in the hall was black and blue with bruises.

In an agony of fear the abbot cried out to the sexton to call the giants off, but the sexton replied that it was useless to tell them to stop until the hiding place of the stolen ball was disclosed.

'It's there, in the chest!' cried the abbot, diving under the table in a vain attempt to escape a blow from one of the huge clubs.

'Give me the key,' demanded the sexton.

Screaming with fright, the abbot dragged the key from his pocket and threw it across the room. The sexton caught it, unlocked the chest, and took out the precious ball which he had been without for so long. As soon as he had it again, the giants went back into their own ball, which at once closed up.

Carrying the small ball under his arm, and trundling the large one in front of him, the sexton returned home gaily. His wife was overjoyed to learn of his good fortune, for now, lacking nothing, they were able to settle down to a quiet and peaceful old age.

But it is the habit of men to grow careless and there came a day when the sexton, wishing to show the miraculous properties of his treasured ball to a company of friends, commanded it to doff its cap without first taking the precaution of seeing that all doors and windows in the room were closed. The door was ajar, and no sooner had the ball begun to roll about the floor than it made across the room, burst through the door, and flew out of the house into the open air. It was followed by the larger ball, which bounded just as swiftly.

Behind them ran the sexton, his wife, and his friends in a vain hue and cry. The balls flew ever faster and faster, until suddenly the smaller one split open. From out of it rushed the troop of dwarfs, carrying with them a great treasure of golden objects of various kinds with which they fled into the mountains.

A moment later the larger ball also split open and the pursuers stopped aghast at the sight of the host of giants which leaped forth from it. For one fearful instant the sexton and his friends expected to be killed, but the giants, after wildly brandishing their clubs, followed the example of the dwarfs and fled pell-mell to the mountains.

The magic balls, like the magic pot, had vanished for ever.

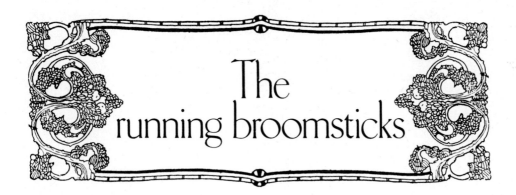

# The running broomsticks

O NCE upon a time there was a kind-hearted cottage woman who was very fond of children, and who would do anything she could to make them happy.

She was very poor, and this troubled her a good deal, because she liked to invite little children to come and stay with her, and it cost more than she could afford to feed them.

One day, as she went to the mill to buy some flour, she took a short cut through a little wood, that was called 'The Fairies' Dell', because the fairies were sometimes to be seen there. And suddenly a lady appeared from behind a tree.

'Martha Motherly,' said the lady, 'I am a fairy, and I have good news for you. From now on you can invite as many little children as you like to your cottage. There will always be food for them, for the cottage cupboard will always be full. You need not go to buy flour now, for there is plenty of flour at home.'

With this the fairy disappeared.

Martha Motherly returned to her cottage and opened the cupboard door. She saw that the fairy had kept her promise. There was plenty of good food in it – better than she could usually buy.

This was a great delight to the good woman, for now she was able to invite as many children as she wished. The news soon got round, and after that the cottage was always full.

Now, the great point about Martha Motherly was not only that she was fond of children and they were fond of her, but hers was the sort of kindness that does children good.

After staying a day or two in her humble little home, any child would seem to be quite changed in manner. Boy or girl, it would go away so sweet-tempered and thoughtful for others, that it would take a long while for the good effect to wear off.

Mothers began to know this, and they would send their children from all the towns and villages round to stay a few nights with Martha Motherly.

Bad-tempered children were sent, boys who tease and girls who cry, and they all came back quite improved, and didn't have to go again for weeks and weeks.

They loved to be in that cottage, and the kind fairy kept her word, and there was always plenty of food for them.

Not far from Martha's cottage there lived a horrid wizard woman who knew all about Martha Motherly's kindness. She knew, too, that the kind fairies were keeping Martha's cupboard full.

'I'll be even with her,' she said. 'I'll see to it that things don't work out for Martha Motherly quite so nicely. People won't want to send their children to her after I've had my time.'

With that the wizard Pettish – for that was her name – dressed herself up to look like a bottle of medicine, and got a lot of other medicine bottles and filled them with nasty things that taste pleasant but that make children cross and quarrelsome, and then she picked out her two magic brooms and wove a spell over them.

After that things began to be a little different at the cottage of Martha Motherly.

It all began with Tommy Feather.

One morning Tommy woke up and declared that everyone was horrid, and that Mrs Motherly was cruel, and that he didn't love anyone, and other things of that sort.

'When I go home I shall pull Cissy's hair,' he said. 'And I shall tease the cat and I shall pinch the baby.'

'But why, Tommy dear?' asked Mrs Motherly.

'I don't know why,' said Tommy; 'but last night I dreamed a funny dream. I chased a sweeping-broom till I came to a cottage, and there a nice lady gave me some lovely stuff out of a bottle. She was ever so much nicer than you.'

And Tommy went home, and was more wicked than he had ever been.

Then the same thing happened to Maggie Fillip. And she told about a queer dream, too, in which she had chased a sweeping-broom, and had seen a lady dressed like a medicine bottle.

And Maggie went home so cross and cruel that no one knew what to do with her.

And then this happened again and again, till hardly a night went by without some child dreaming about running brooms, and then being ever so cross and naughty for days afterwards.

Of course Martha Motherly was greatly upset. She knew that if this went on fathers and mothers would begin to hear about it, and would not let their children come to her cottage. And to have no dear little children round her would have broken her heart.

So she went to the kind fairy and told her all about it.

'Cheer up,' said the fairy. 'I think I know what is happening. You must ask little Nellie

Manners to come and stay with you. She is a sweet-natured little girl, and she is under the protection of the fairies, so that no wizard can hurt her.'

Martha Motherly had often heard of little Nellie Manners, and of her sweet nature and kind deeds. So she thanked the fairy, and set off to call at Blue Hill farm, where Nellie lived.

Nellie heard the story of what was happening to the children, and what queer dreams they all had about the running sweeping-brooms, and she gladly promised to come. And her mother, from whom she had learned many of her kind ways, was quite willing for her to do so.

That evening Nellie came, and a bed was found for her. But Nellie did not mean to fall asleep if she could help it.

Suddenly in the middle of the night she heard a queer sound and saw a strange sight.

Two sweeping-brushes were having a dance in the middle of the room.

Then the other sweeping-broom stopped before Nellie's bed a moment and started for the door. Nellie bounced out and chased after it.

Out of the cottage she went, out into a dark valley down by a stream, and the broom ran in front. Right ahead she saw Daisy chasing the other broom.

On they went for a long way, then into a shed by one door and out by another, and there was a cottage on a little hill. On the wall sat Daisy talking to an old lady dressed like a medicine bottle, with her white apron labelled 'poison'.

Nellie knew in a moment that this woman was a wizard woman. She saw Daisy follow her into the house. Through the open door she saw the wizard woman climb on the top of some books to reach a shelf of medicine bottles.

Then Nellie rushed in and caught hold of Daisy and pushed her out. She took hold of the broom that Daisy had followed, and sat on the floor behind the wizard woman. The moment she touched the broom the legs disappeared and the stockings fell off.

The wizard woman turned around.

'Bless me! You are different child!' she cried.

'And you are a naughty wizard woman,' replied Nellie.

At this the wizard woman grew very angry.

'You are not the child I want!' she cried. 'Go away!'

Suddenly one of them leaned over a girl called Daisy Donner, and beckoned to her. Up got Daisy. The broom hopped out of the room, Daisy following.

Nellie saw that the broom had a little pair of feet and could run, also that it had gathered up a pair of stockings, which waved like arms.

And as she said the words her eyes opened wide, and a frightened look came into her face.

'Let go of my broom!' she said. 'Let go of the sweeping-brush! You are spoiling my magic. Do you want to rob me of all my magic powers?'

'Yes, I do,' replied Nellie.

And then a sudden idea seized her, and she lifted up the broom and brought it down, smash! smash! smash! on all the bottles.

At this the wizard woman uttered a terrible cry.

'You have spoiled all my magic,' she cried, 'and I can never be a wizard woman any more! For if a wizard's broomstick is used to spoil a single spell, that ends it all.'

At once she changed back into her usual shape, instead of looking like a medicine bottle.

'Now I'm nothing but a poor old woman!' she sobbed. 'And I shall have to work hard at washing and ironing.'

Of course, Nellie didn't feel very sorry for her. Why should she? The wizard woman was so wicked.

She hurried out of the cottage, and found Daisy outside, rubbing her eyes.

'How did I get her?' asked Daisy.

Nellie told her, and brought her back to Martha Motherly's cottage.

And that ended the work of the wicked wizard woman. After that more children than ever came to Martha's home, so that sometimes she had to put out notices such as 'No more babies wanted' and 'House full'. People had to take turns, and often wait a week or more before they could send their little ones to stay.

Nellie often came across to spend a night out and help amuse the children, and you may be sure that she was always welcome.

The old wizard woman did not stay in that place long, because people got to know she was a wizard who had lost her powers, so she had to move away into mountain land, where she lived by keeping goats.

# The magic scissors and thimble

ONCE there was a peasant who was so poor that he had much difficulty in bringing up his three sons. As soon as each was old enough to work, therefore, he had to start earning a living.

The eldest, being a strapping lad, was quickly apprenticed to a blacksmith, who was a friend of the family.

The second boy was not so sturdy, and as it seemed unlikely that he would be able to cope with the hard labour of the blacksmith's trade he was apprenticed to a locksmith, whom the elder brother's master knew.

The case of the third son was difficult, for he was not only less vigorous than the other two but he grew up such a small shrimp of a fellow that his parents were at their wits' end to know what to do with him. The only occupation which they could find for him was tending their few geese.

However, one day a Wise Woman came to the cottage to beg for a cup of water and a little bread. The peasant's wife, who had heard of the magic powers her visitor was supposed to have, asked for advice about her youngest son, in return for such poor hospitality as she had been able to offer.

'Let him be a tailor,' said the Wise Woman. 'It is a trade for which he is well suited, and in which, mark my words, he will make his fortune. See, here is a thimble for him. Give it to your son when he returns home, for it will serve him well.'

As the Wise Woman was about to go, little Hans returned with his flock of geese. His mother at once called him to her and put into his hands the thimble which she had just received from her visitor.

Hans, who had a gentle nature, turned to the old woman and thanked her politely for her valuable gift. This so pleased her that she produced from the bag which hung at her side a pair of scissors, which she also gave to Hans. Then she added a word of advice.

'Be sure never to part with either thimble or scissors,' she said. 'Never work with any others, and all will go well with you.'

Next day Hans took the scissors and thimble in his pocket, and went to a tailor's shop in the neighbouring village. He asked the tailor for employment, and was told to sit down, and let it be seen how well he could sew.

The boy at once slipped on the magic thimble, and with its help sewed so well that the tailor was astonished, and immediately offered to take Hans as an apprentice.

Before long the tailor began to instruct his new apprentice in the art of cutting out clothes, but Hans produced his magic scissors, and with their help showed such skill that tuition was hardly necessary.

The tailor was delighted; never before had such a clever boy been apprenticed to him. In

the course of as many weeks as should ordinarily have been years, Hans' apprenticeship was declared to be at an end, and he became the tailor's chief assistant.

Soon Hans determined to try his fortune in the wide world. So he took the road and journeyed to the nearest town.

At first no one would give him employment, for he did not look his age. At last he took a job with the poor widow of a tailor, who was trying with little success to carry on her late husband's business.

This woman quickly discovered the boy's cleverness, and before long Hans was made foreman over the workmen she employed. The latter were green with envy, and no wonder, for they had been many years at work, and resented their new young master. Hans took no notice of their discontent, but went on with his work.

But presently the workmen noticed that Hans could never be persuaded to use any thimble or scissors except his own. They therefore plotted to steal them.

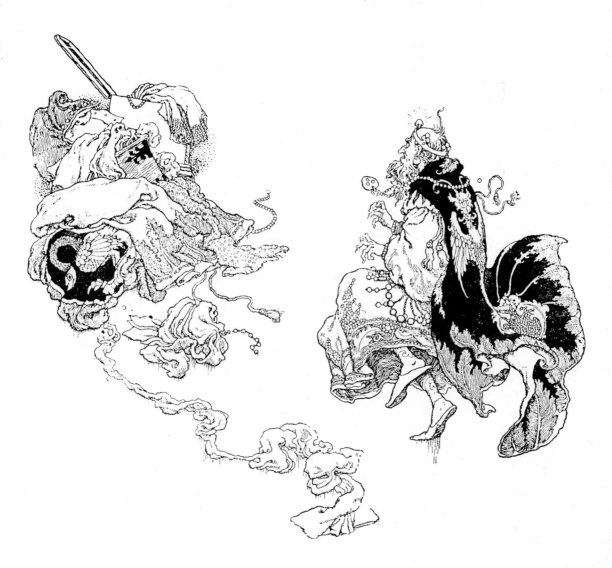

One day when Hans had left the workshop for a short time, a workman seized the scissors, which he had left on his bench, and began to cut out a coat.

To the man's astonishment the scissors went by themselves, his hand merely following them, and in a trice the coat was cut out more quickly than the astonished workman had ever thought possible. But when he unfolded the cloth, and began to arrange the pieces, he was horrified to find that the garment was shaped for a hunchback, and that one sleeve was much longer than the other.

Terrified, the thieving workman flung the scissors away, and called his fellows to see for themselves the trick which had been played on him. At once there was uproar in the workshop. The tailors said that their foreman was guilty of witchcraft, and loudly declared their intention to bring him to justice.

In the midst of all the turmoil Hans returned unobserved. Overhearing what was said, he determined to leave before there was any more trouble. Taking back his scissors and thimble, he ran away the same night, and travelled in search of new fortunes.

In due course the young tailor reached another town. Entering by the nearest gate, he was astonished to find all the people in the streets were dressed in sackcloth, mostly black in colour.

Suspicious looks were turned on him, and he had not gone very far up the street before two men dressed in red sackcloth, who seemed to be constables or officers of some kind, took hold of him roughly. They demanded who and what he was, and on Hans replying that he was a stranger who had just arrived, and a tailor by trade, they dragged him off to the court-house.

Presently he was brought before the town elders, who sat in state on a bench covered in black meal-sacks.

'Who and what are you?' demanded the chief of the elders. 'And what are you doing here dressed like this?'

'My name is Hans, and my trade is that of a tailor,' replied the astonished youth. 'As for my clothes,' he added, rather offended, 'they are the latest fashion.'

'Unhappy youth!' said the chief elder. 'Do you not know that it is unlawful for any tailor to enter this town, or for any clothing except sackcloth to be worn within it? For the latter offence you are condemned to one hundred lashes; for daring to come here, although a tailor, you will be compelled to a trial of strength with the Giant who keeps guard over our Sovereign's daughter. If you should defeat the Giant, your reward will be the hand of the Princess, but should you fail your lot is death.'

In vain did Hans plead ignorance of the strange laws belonging to the town which he had so rashly entered. No excuse softened his stern judges, and the poor fellow was led away and thrown into gaol. The only consolation allowed to him was that since he must face the Giant, the flogging he was to be given for wearing the wrong clothes would be postponed.

In no way worried by the prospect of the strange adventure in store for him, Hans thought himself lucky to have escaped the flogging, if only for the present, and smilingly followed his guard.

For two days he remained in prison, and the gaoler, having pity on the lad, spent much time talking to him. Hans was not long in asking how such a strange state of affairs had come to pass in the city.

'My trade is an honourable one,' he said, 'and I do not understand why it should be held in such disfavour. Why, also, should it be thought necessary for everyone to go about in sackcloth, which, to say the least, is not a flattering outfit?'

'It is because of the vanity of women,' said the gaoler. 'The trouble began with the late Queen, who was much too fond of clothes. Every day of her life she had a new dress made for her, and, as you may well suppose, she had

time to think of little else. This was bad enough, but her daughter inherited the vice in a still worse degree.

'Things were no better when at last the Queen died, for when the Princess began to grow up she proved herself far worse. Not one, but seven dresses had to be made for her every day, and she spent the whole of her time putting them on and taking them off.

'At last things reached such a pitch that the King, her father, lost all patience. He shut the Princess up in a lonely tower, and set a Giant to watch over her. At the same time he made a proclamation requiring that all the inhabitants of the city should wear sackcloth for ever more, and banished every tailor. In future no tailor was allowed to enter the city, and you have already heard the penalties for breaking this law.'

At last the day of the contest with the Giant

W. HEATH ROBINSON

arrived, and Hans was led by his guards into the forest. When they reached a spot near the Giant's lair, and could hear the latter snoring, the guards retired, telling Hans to go forward.

In some fear Hans followed the path alone. Suddenly there stood before him the Wise Woman from whom he had received the thimble and the scissors which had helped him so much.

'Be of good cheer, my son,' said the old dame; 'take with you this hedgehog and this bird, for you will find them useful.'

The astonished Hans had scarcely received these new gifts and pushed them into his wallet when the Wise Woman vanished.

Much cheered, Hans continued on his way. Presently he saw the huge shape of the Giant coming towards him through the trees, whilst from over the treetops came a terrible voice.

'You miserable dwarf! Do you dare to pit your puny strength against mine? Come hither to the bowling-green, and see which of us can send a bowl the farthest.'

Hans made his way through the trees to where the Giant awaited him at the end of a long green lawn. The Giant picked up a bowl, and sent it trundling down the green alley. It rolled and rolled until Hans began to think it would never stop. Just as it was vanishing from his eyes it came to a standstill.

Trying to look as confident as possible, Hans put his hand into his wallet, and pulled out the hedgehog which the Wise Woman had given him. He swung his arm as though about to throw a bowl, and in so doing dropped the hedgehog on the grass.

The little creature at once started off along the bowling-green. It travelled more slowly than the Giant's bowl, but it travelled steadily. In due course it passed the spot where the Giant's bowl had come to rest, and scurried away out of sight.

'You have won, this time!' said the Giant angrily. 'Show me now if you can throw as well as you can trundle.'

Followed by Hans, he strode through the forest to where a tall tower, many storeys high, stood in a clearing.

'Watch now,' said the Giant, 'and see me strike the topmost storey.'

Picking up a stone he flung it into the air. It landed on the tower a storey lower than he had boastfully anticipated, but that was high enough to dishearten a less plucky competitor than Hans.

The latter put his hand once more into his wallet, and this time took out the Wise Woman's bird. Pretending it was a stone, he flung it into the air. The bird flew swiftly up, high over the tower, and disappeared into the blue sky.

'You are strong in the arms,' admitted the Giant grudgingly. 'Let me see now what you can do with your legs.'

So saying he sprang into the air and leapt over a tall oak that stood nearby.

'That is not so bad,' said Hans coolly, when the Giant returned. 'Before I make my effort, kindly pull down for me the top of this poplar, for I wish to measure the height of the jump I am going to make.'

The unsuspecting Giant bent the high poplar until Hans was able to catch hold of the topmost boughs. As soon as he had a firm grasp on them he called out to his opponent: 'You may let go now, for I have taken the measurement.'

The Giant let go the poplar, which at once sprang back to its original position, and Hans, holding tight to the topmost boughs, was carried up into the air. At the critical moment he let go, and thus was able to make an amazing leap, which completely eclipsed the performance of the Giant.

'You have won the day,' cried the Giant. 'Your life is spared, and the King's daughter is yours.'

He hoisted Hans on to his shoulder, so that through the window of one of the upper storeys of the tower he could see the Princess inside. At once Hans threw open the window, went into the Princess's apartment, and led her to the Royal presence. He told the King how he had defeated the Giant, and as he had promised the monarch gave up his throne and his daughter to the tailor.

Thus the little tailor became a King, and if there is truth in the rumour, he used his magic scissors to cut good men out of bad, and his thimble to sew on the legs and arms which his gallant soldiers sometimes lost in the battles which they fought for him.

# The three faithful companions

HERE was once a King who was very old, and had only one son. One day he called the Prince and said:

'My dear son, before I die I would like to see my future daughter, your wife, so you must get married.'

The Prince answered:

'I would be happy to fulfil your wish, my father, but as yet I have no bride. I do not know one.'

The King put his hand into his pocket and took from it a golden key, which he gave to his son, saying:

'Go up into the highest room in the tower, and when you are there look round you, and tell me which of the brides whom you will see there pleases you the most.'

When the Prince reached the highest room but one he saw in the ceiling a small iron door like a lid, which was locked; but he unlocked it with the golden key, lifted it up, and went through it.

There was a large, round room, the roof of which was as blue as the sky on a clear winter's night, and silver stars glittered on it. The floor was covered with a green silken carpet, and the room had twelve high windows in golden framework. In each window was painted, in the loveliest colours, a beautiful lady, with a Royal crown on her head, but each one was more beautiful than the other, so that the

Prince was quite dazzled. As he was gazing on them in astonishment, not knowing which to choose, the lovely figures began to move like living things, and looked at him and smiled at him, as if they wished to speak.

Then the Prince saw that one of the windows was hidden by a white curtain, which he drew aside in order to see what was behind it.

There stood a maiden dressed in white, with a silver girdle round her waist and a crown of pearls on her head. She was the loveliest of all, but sad and pale. The Prince stood gazing at the figure for a long time, as though he were in a trance, and while he was looking at her he said: 'She and no other shall be my choice.' As soon as he had spoken the lady bent her head, and a flush spread over her cheeks. At the same moment all the other figures vanished.

After the Prince had left the tower and returned to the King, he told his father all that he had seen and which of the ladies he had chosen. Then the old King was filled with sorrow, and said:

'You have chosen ill, my son, and done wrong in uncovering what was concealed. You will meet with great dangers, because of the words which you have spoken. This maiden is in the power of a wicked enchanter and imprisoned in an iron castle, and none of those who have gone to set her free have ever returned to their homes.'

The Prince now rode out in search of the

iron castle, so that he might rescue his bride. When he had gone a long way and was wandering in a wood, he heard a voice behind him shout:

'Hallo, there! Stop!'

The Prince turned round and saw a tall man hurrying towards him.

'Wait and take me with you,' said the voice. 'If you take me into your service, you will never have cause to repent it.'

'Who are you?' said the Prince. 'And what can you do?'

'My name is Longfellow, and I can stretch out my limbs to a great length. Do you see the bird's nest at the top of that high fir tree? I can reach it down for you without having to climb the tree.'

So saying, he began to stretch himself out, and his body became longer and longer till he was as high as the tree itself. Then he reached out to take the nest, and when he had taken it his body shrank again, and he handed the nest to the Prince.

'You understand your business well,' said the Prince. 'But what is the use of birds' nests to me, if you cannot help me out of the forest?'

'That is easy enough,' replied Longfellow; and he stretched himself again, until he was three times as high as the tallest tree in the forest. He then looked round and, pointing in a certain direction, said: 'On that side is the nearest road out of the wood.'

Then he drew himself in again, took the horse by the bridle, and went on in front.

'There goes my companion,' said Longfellow, pointing to a figure in the distance. 'You ought to take him with you, too, for he could be very useful to you.'

'Call him, then,' said the Prince, 'so that I can see what there is in him.'

'I would rather go and fetch him,' answered Longfellow.

Then Longfellow lengthened himself again towards the sky, till his head reached the clouds, made one or two steps, seized his comrade by the arm, and placed him before the Prince. He was a broad, muscular fellow.

'Who are you?' asked the Prince. 'And what can you do?'

'Master, I am called Broadfellow, and I can swell myself out to a great breadth.'

'Let me see,' said the Prince, 'what you can do.'

'Ride as fast as you can into the forest,' replied Broadfellow. And immediately he began to swell himself out.

The Prince was puzzled to know why he should ride away so quickly, but when he saw Longfellow running with all his might towards the forest, he spurred on his horse and hurried after him. And it was lucky for him that he did so, or Broadfellow would soon have crushed him and his horse to death, for he grew so quickly on all sides that the whole place was soon filled with him. Then he stopped swelling himself, and blew out the air with such force that he made the forest shake, and appeared again as before.

'You have put me in a difficult position,' said the Prince, 'but a fellow like you is not to be found every day, so come along with me.'

As they went on their way they met a man with his eyes bandaged.

'This is our other comrade,' said Longfellow. 'You ought to take him into your service, for he will be useful.'

'Who are you?' demanded the Prince. 'And why are your eyes bound? Surely you cannot see your way?'

'On the contrary, sir,' he replied, 'it is just because I see too clearly that I have my eyes bound, for with them bound I can see as well as you can with yours free. If I take off the bandage my sight pierces through the thickest substance; and if I look rather hard at anything it either takes fire or flies into a thousand pieces. For this reason I am called Keeneye.'

He then turned towards some rocks opposite, removed the bandage, and fixed his fiery eyes steadily on them. Presently the hard rocks began to crackle, the pieces flew in all directions, and in a few moments nothing was left of the rocks but a heap of sand. Then they saw in the midst of the sand something shining like fire. Keeneye fetched it and presented it to the Prince, who, on beholding it, found that it was a lump of pure gold.

'You are indeed a valuable fellow,' said the Prince. 'It would be stupid not to make use of your services. But since you have such an excellent eye, look and tell me how far we are from the iron castle, and what is going on in it at this moment.'

'If you ride along, master,' answered Keeneye, 'you would not arrive there in a year; but with our help you will be there before the day is over. They are at this moment preparing the evening meal for us.'

'And what is my bride doing?' asked the Prince.

> 'She is sitting alone
> In the gloomy tower,
> Cruelly bound
> By magic power.'

'Then,' said the Prince, 'let whoever is my friend help me to set her free.'

And they all promised to help him. So they journeyed on, and shortly afterwards they crossed the iron bridge that led to the old castle gate. As soon as they had passed through, the bridge raised itself, the gates closed, and they stood prisoners in the iron castle.

Everything was prepared for them, and when they entered the castle hall they saw by the twilight many people in gorgeous clothes, both men and women, but not one of them moved. They were all turned to stone.

After wandering through many apartments the Prince and his companions came at last to the banquet hall. It was brilliantly lit and in the middle stood a table covered with rich food and laid for four persons. Finding that no one appeared, they sat down and began to eat and drink till they were satisfied. When they had finished their meal they looked about to see if they could find some place to sleep.

Suddenly the door flew open, and the enchanter walked into the room. He was an old man, dressed in a long black robe, and bowed down by years. His head was bald, but his grey beard flowed down to his knees, and instead of a girdle three iron rings surrounded his body. He led by the hand a most lovely Princess, clothed in white. Around her waist she wore a silver girdle, and on her head a crown of pearls; but she was pale and sad, as though she had been crying.

The Prince knew her again in a moment, and sprang up and went towards her, but he was stopped by the enchanter who addressed him in these words:

'I know why you have come hither; your intention is to bear away this Princess. Good. Be it so. It is permitted you to claim her after you have guarded her for three nights together without allowing her to escape. If you fail, you and your three attendants shall be turned into stone, like all those who have made the attempt before you.'

He then led the Princess to a seat and went away.

The Prince could not turn away his eyes from her, she was so very lovely. He began to speak to her and to ask her many things; but she did not answer, nor did she even smile or look at him, but remained like a marble statue. He sat down by her side and resolved not to sleep during the whole of the night, so that she might not escape.

For greater safety Longfellow lengthened himself to his fullest extent, and lay all round the room; Broadfellow placed himself in the doorway, swelled out his body, and stopped the way so completely that even a mouse could not get through; and Keeneye stood in the middle of the room like a pillar, so as to keep watch. In a little while, however, all three, growing weary, fell asleep, and slept the whole night as soundly as if they had been at the bottom of the ocean.

When the morning light began to dawn the Prince awoke first, and when he saw that the Princess had disappeared he felt as though he had been struck with a knife. He lost no time in arousing the three companions, and asked what was to be done.

'Do not be in the least troubled, master,' said Keeneye, looking out of the window, 'for I see her already. A hundred miles from this castle is a forest. In the middle of that forest stands an oak; on that oak is an acorn, and that acorn is the Princess. Longfellow shall take me on his shoulders, and we will soon get her back again.'

So he got upon Longfellow's shoulders, who stretched himself out and left the castle. Each step he took measured ten miles. Keeneye showed him the way, and in less time than it takes to go round a cottage they were back again. Longfellow gave the acorn to the Prince and said:

'Let it fall upon the ground.'

The Prince did as he was told, and at the same moment the beautiful Princess stood before him.

As the sun began to show itself above the hills the door flew open with a loud crash, and the magician entered, with a fiendish laugh; but as soon as he saw the Princess there he became gloomy. As he was muttering something between his teeth, one of the three rings that were around his waist snapped and fell to the ground. He then took the Princess by the hand and led her away.

The next day the Prince, having nothing to do, wandered through the castle and all round to see everything that was most remarkable there. On all sides it seemed as if life had stopped short at one blow.

At morning, noon, and evening the Prince and his companions found a sumptuous meal ready for them. An unseen hand served up the food and poured the wine into their glasses, so that they had nothing to do but to eat and drink.

Scarcely was the evening meal over before the door opened and the magician again appeared, leading the Princess who was to be guarded a second night by the Prince. Now, although they had firmly made up their minds to keep awake this night, it was of no use, for soon the Prince and his companions fell into a sound slumber. And when at early dawn the Prince awoke and found the Princess gone again, he sprang up, and, seizing Keeneye by the shoulder, cried:

'Ho, there! Wake up, Keeneye! Do you know where the lady has gone?'

Keeneye rubbed his eyes a little while, then looked round him and said:

'I already see her. Two hundred miles from here stands a hill. Inside that hill is a rock. Inside that rock is a precious stone, and that precious stone is the Princess. If Longfellow will carry me on his shoulders, we will soon get her back.'

Longfellow then took his comrade on his shoulders, lengthened himself out, and left the castle. Each step he took measured twenty miles. When they arrived within sight of the hill, Keeneye fixed his fiery eye on it, and immediately it began to crumble, and the rock became a burning mass, in the midst of which the precious stone was seen to glitter. They took it up and brought it to the Prince, and as soon as he had thrown it on the ground the Princess stood again before him. When the magician came and saw her there, his eyes flashed with anger, and before he had time to speak a second ring snapped and fell from his body. The magician growled with rage and led the Princess away.

This day passed like the one before it. After the evening meal the magician brought in the Princess again, and looking with a keen glance into the Prince's eye said, with a fiendish chuckle:

'It will now be seen which is the mightier of us two – whether you or I will gain the victory.'

Whereupon he left the room, and all three, being determined not to sleep that night, resolved not even to sit down; but in spite of their efforts one after the other they fell asleep even while walking. And the Princess escaped a third time.

In the morning the Prince was again the first to discover the disappearance of the Princess. He ran to his keen-eyed companion and, shaking him violently, cried:

'Ho, Keeneye! Get up and tell me where the Princess is.'

Keeneye stood looking for a long time.

'I see her at last,' he said. 'She is a long way off, master – a very long way off. Three hundred miles from here is the Black Sea. In the middle of the sea, lying at the bottom, is a mussel; in the middle of that mussel is a golden ring. That ring is the Princess. Do not be troubled, master, for we shall get her back; but we shall have to take Broadfellow with us this time, for we shall want him.'

Longfellow then, taking Keeneye on one shoulder and Broadfellow on the other, started on his way. Each step he took measured thirty miles.

When they came to the Black Sea, Keeneye showed his companion what part of the sea the mussel was to be found in. Longfellow stretched out his hand as far as he was able, but could not reach the bottom.

'Stop, comrades, stop a little,' exclaimed Broadfellow, 'and let me help you!'

When he had spoken these words he began swelling himself as far as he could. He then lay down on the shore and began to drink. As he drank, the water fell, until at last it was low enough to allow Longfellow to reach the bottom easily, and to bring up the ring.

Meanwhile, in the castle the Prince was growing very uneasy. The dawn was already breaking, and his attendants were not yet back. In a moment the door flew open and the magician appeared in the doorway. When he saw that the Princess was not there, a grin of malicious delight spread over his face, but before he could utter a word the window was smashed into a thousand pieces, the ring fell on the ground, and the Princess stood before them! For Keeneye, when he saw what was going on in the castle, told Longfellow what great danger his master stood in. Longfellow then made one rapid step, and, stretching out his arm, threw the ring through the window into the room. The magician roared with anger, so that the castle trembled. In an instant a third ring snapped and fell to the ground, and at the same time the magician was transformed into a raven, and flew away through the broken window.

Then the beautiful Princess began to speak, and as she thanked the Prince for her freedom a soft blush spread over her cheeks.

Everything in all parts of the castle was filled with life. Each of the stone figures finished what he was about to do before the words of the magician turned him into a statue.

The Prince now began to think of returning to his father's palace with his bride and his faithful companions. They all started out, and at last arrived.

The old King wept for joy at the good fortune of his son, and three weeks later the happy wedding took place in the palace chapel.

When it was over the comrades told the Prince that they wished to go again into the wide world to seek employment.

The Prince tried to persuade them to stay.

'I will give you whatever you wish till you die, and you will have no need to work.'

But they were not content with such an idle life so they went away, and are still wandering about in some part of the world.

# The idle fellow

ONCE upon a time there was a man who had three sons. The two eldest were both clever fellows, and had married wives, but the youngest was extremely lazy and stupid, so much so that no one ever called him anything but the Dolt, or the Idle Fellow.

When the father felt his end approaching he divided his wealth between his eldest sons. Then he gave to each boy the additional sum of a hundred ducats, and died.

One day the two brothers said to the Dolt: 'Give us your hundred ducats. We are going on a great journey, which will make us very wealthy, and we will bring you back a red cap, a red belt, and some red slippers. While we are away you must stay with our wives and do as they tell you.'

For a long time the Dolt had wanted the things which his brothers now promised him, and he immediately handed over all his money. He then settled down at home in the company of his sisters-in-law, and, being the most idle fellow that ever was seen, spent all his time sitting down or stretched out before the stove, never getting up except in a temper to answer a call from the women. Indeed, the latter, in order to make him obey, were obliged to tempt him with hot soup, biscuits, or sweet wine, for otherwise he refused to do anything at all.

'Get up, idle fellow,' they said to him one day. 'Go and fetch some water.'

The Dolt did not stir. It was freezing as hard as possible, and he did not like the idea of going out.

'Go and do it yourselves,' he replied.

'If you hurry up, silly boy, we will give you some wine and biscuits when you get back; but if you don't we shall complain of you to our husbands when they return, and you will get neither cap, belt, nor slippers.'

The Idle Fellow got up, took the pitchers and a hatchet, and went down to the river, where he broke the ice and filled his buckets. Then he stood still for a moment watching the stream run by. Suddenly he saw a pike which was swimming close to the bank. He quickly plunged his arm into the river, and without any difficulty caught the fish.

'Throw me back into the water,' said the pike, 'and I will give you whatever you wish.'

'Will you, indeed? Then I want whatever I wish for to come true at once.'

'Very good. You have only to say, "I desire, on the word of a pike, that such-and-such a thing may happen."'

The Dolt agreed to set the fish free, and watched it dive to the bottom of the stream.

Then he turned towards the two buckets of water.

'I desire, on the word of a pike, that these pails carry themselves to the house,' he said.

The buckets walked away immediately, and

the Idle Fellow followed them, with a stick in his hand, driving them as if they had been geese. In this way he returned home with not a thought in his head except to get back to his place by the stove.

'Now then, Idle Fellow,' said his sisters-in-law a moment later, 'take a hatchet and go and cut some wood.'

'Not me! Do it yourselves.'

'If you don't go at once we shall let the stove go out, and you will shiver with cold.'

As soon as they had gone, the Dolt shifted slightly, and said: 'I desire, on the word of a pike, that the wood may be cut.'

Immediately the hatchet came out of its cupboard, dashed off to the shed and chopped the wood, and the latter came of its own accord and put itself on the fire. All the time the Idle Fellow was stretched comfortably on his bench close to the stove, sleeping peacefully.

Some days later the two women again called out to the Dolt:

'There is no more wood in the house. Go and find some in the forest.'

This time the lad made no protest, being pleased by the thought that all the village would now see what he could do. He took some biscuits and a bottle of wine, and went to look for the sledge. There was no horse to harness to it, but he did not worry over such a trifle as that. Taking a long whip off its hook, he cried out:

'I desire, on the word of a pike, that this sledge shall go of its own accord.'

No sooner said than done! In this vehicle the Dolt passed through a large village, and the people ran from every side to watch the sledge that went without a horse. In ever-increasing numbers they crowded round the strange carriage, showering the lad with questions and trying to stop him. Eventually they began to annoy him, and in order to escape their curiosity he went even faster, terrifying the women and children, upsetting the dogs, and causing a great commotion.

When he reached the forest he took all the wood he wanted, and returned by the same road to get home. But in going through the village where, some hours earlier, he had been the cause of so much chaos, he was seized by the peasants, who stopped his sledge and took him into custody. He seemed in for an awkward time, when an idea struck him.

'I desire, on the word of a pike, that the sticks on my sledge shall give a beating to all these people.'

At once the sticks fell upon the backs, the shoulders, and the legs of the peasants, who ran away with howls of terror.

Rumour of his exploits eventually reached the ears of the King, who was curious to meet the lad, and told one of his captains to bring the worker of miracles before him. The captain went to the house of the Dolt's sisters-in-law, and explained his errand to them.

'Here, Idle Fellow,' cried the two women, 'come out of your snug corner and go to the King's Court. Put on your Sunday clothes quickly, and be off without delay.'

'Follow me to the court,' said the messenger, 'for the King desires to present you with a red cap, a red belt, and some red slippers.'

The Idle Fellow, highly delighted, said to the envoy:

'I will go this moment. Get on your way at once, for I shall be there before you.' Then he added, in a lower voice, 'I desire, on the word of a pike, that the stove by which I am seated shall carry me to the King's Court.'

As he uttered the words the stove went cold, placed itself between the Idle Fellow's legs, and dashed off along the road.

Comfortably seated on this strange vehicle, the lad munched biscuits and drank a bottle of good wine, until the stove stopped before the steps of the palace. The King and his courtiers happened to be on the balcony, and they were filled with amazement at this extraordinary spectacle.

'Who are you?' cried the King. 'And what

do you want?'

'I am the Dolt, or the Idle Fellow, whichever you please, and I have come to claim my slippers, my cap, and my belt.'

As he spoke he raised his head and perceived at a window the King's daughter, who was of dazzling beauty.

'I desire, on the word of a pike,' he whispered, 'that this charming princess may become my wife.' Then he went off as he had come.

Sure enough, the King's daughter suddenly fell in love with this man whom she had scarcely seen. The King, in despair, had the

Dolt arrested. He was brought to the Palace
and handed to a magician.

The magician shut him up in a huge crystal
barrel, where he soon went to sleep, but the
King's daughter came on the scene just at that
moment and implored her father to allow her
to share the fate of the man whom she loved.
Furious, the King gave orders that his daughter
should be shut up with the Dolt, so that he
might never hear another word from her. This
was done, and the barrel flew up into the air.

After a while the Princess woke the Idle Fellow, and asked if he could save them.

'Of course I can,' he answered. 'I desire, on the word of a pike, that we find ourselves this very moment in a beautiful castle.'

The barrel gently landed the two travellers, and all they had to do was to walk at once into a magnificent marble palace. The Princess begged her lover to go with her to the Court of her father the King, in order to ask his pardon and beg his blessing.

Then it occurred to the Dolt that he, the

stupidest man in all the kingdom, was not really worthy to become the husband of this beautiful Princess. Under his breath he uttered his final wish: 'I desire, on the word of a pike, that I may be filled with wit and wisdom.'

At once he became as brilliant in wit as he had been stupid, and as energetic as he had been idle. He took the Princess by the hand and went with her, as she had wished, to the King's Court. There the couple threw themselves at the monarch's feet, and the young man pleaded his cause so well that the King gave him his daughter's hand.

A splendid wedding took place, and the young couple lived happily ever after.

# Prince Roshun

ONG ago, by the banks of Mai Gunga, Holy Mother Ganges, stretched a great kingdom, bounded on its northern side by the dense jungle called the Terai. The king of this land had three sons, all of whom were strong and handsome.

The youngest, however, was by far the best-looking, and had the sweetest nature.

He was called Prince Roshun (Brightness), and was a favourite with everybody.

The King, his father, seemed to treat the Prince very unkindly. While his elder brothers had beautiful garments, and turbans of soft silk set off by sparkling diamonds, Prince Roshun wore the simplest clothes and possessed no jewels. They had horses and attendants, but he went on foot, followed only by a pet monkey. In spite of this the three princes were devoted to each other, and the elder brothers always tried to share their toys and amusements with 'Chotoo', as they affectionately called their little brother.

The day came when the two elder princes were thought to be of the right age for marriage, and messengers were sent to the kings of neighbouring lands to ask if they had daughters beautiful and wealthy enough to marry the princes.

At last two princesses were chosen, and preparations for the weddings began. Elephants laden with gifts from the princes – golden anklets hung with tiny bells that jingled as the wearer moved, bracelets, rings set with tiny mirrors, muslins so delicately woven that they looked as fine as a spider's web, silken veils embroidered with the wings of dragon-flies, and slippers sewn with pearls – were dispatched to the future brides, and from them came in return swords of wonderfully wrought steel in gem-studded scabbards, and pictures of themselves in carved ivory cases.

'Where is the bride of Prince Roshun? Why is he not to be married at the same time as his brothers?' the people asked each other, and at last a high official repeated their words to the King.

'I have enough wealth to provide for two sons during my lifetime, and at my death they shall rule together over this kingdom; but Roshun must seek his own fortune!' replied the King harshly.

The night of the wedding arrived, and the palace was bright with lights and merry with music. In a tiny room high in a turret Prince Roshun sat sadly, with only his monkey beside him. He had been sternly forbidden to join the merry-making.

Far down the road he saw the flicker of torches and heard the gay drumming, and soon two litters hung with cloth of gold were carried into the courtyard of the palace.

When they had been set down, servant-girls ran out of the palace, carrying rolls of scarlet

cloth, with which they made a closed-in pathway for the brides to pass along without being seen by curious eyes.

Roshun caught a glimpse of two slim, veiled figures glittering with jewels, but the next instant the princesses had entered the palace and the scarlet cloth was being rolled up again.

'Alas!' said the Prince aloud. 'If only I could find a beautiful young bride too!'

At that moment he felt a skinny hand on his knee, and, looking down, he saw the wizened face of his monkey. It looked at him, and then out of the window to where, dark and silent, the edge of the jungle appeared beyond the palace grounds.

'What! You want to go hunting at this time of night!' said Roshun. 'Very well, Laloo. We will go together to seek a fortune and a princess whom I can marry. Perhaps I shall find one beyond the dreadful jungle.'

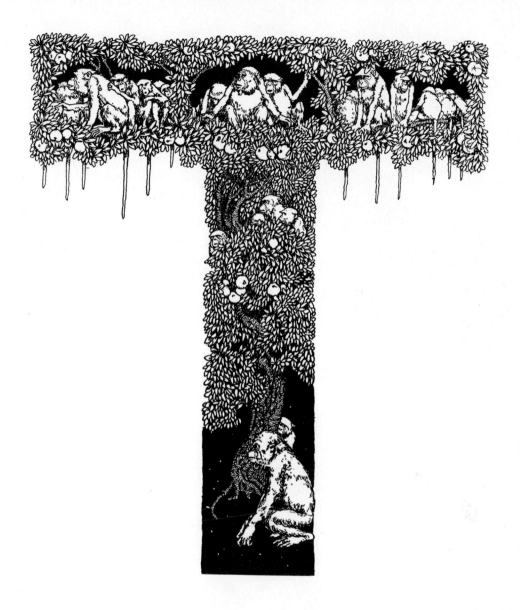

He tied some food in a bundle, and then, taking a strong staff in his hand, he made his way out of the palace by empty corridors, Laloo, the monkey, following close on his heels. They crossed the beautiful grounds of the palace and went along the dusty, silent road. Every minute the jungle loomed darker and nearer. Soon they were passing under the tall trees, brushing past dangling creepers and listening to the scuttling away of many ani-mals. The Prince now became aware that the monkey was in front, leading the way.

He followed meekly, feeling surprised at Laloo's courage, because the monkey, as a rule, dreaded the darkness and clung to his master.

On, on they went, till at last the monkey stopped in a clearing near a pool of water and gave a low, wailing call.

The next instant the Prince heard the patter of small feet and the crashing of branches and

twigs, and became aware that the trees around him were alive with monkeys of all shapes and sizes. There were great gorilla-like animals that stood up like human beings, black-faced baboons, monkeys with a fringe of white hair round their faces, and other little shivering brown ones.

His surprise was doubled when he heard Laloo speaking to them.

'My people,' he said, 'I have called you here so that you may see and know this prince. If ever he is in danger, protect him; if ever in need, help him.' The monkeys chattered excitedly, and then swung away into the darkness. Then Laloo turned to the Prince.

'We will now look for your bride,' he said. 'She is hidden in the lotus-bud floating on that pool. Pick it, and carry it carefully, but do not touch its petals till they open of themselves.'

The Prince picked the lotus-bud and carried it carefully. They went on through the forest, and at last they entered the land on its far side. The Prince saw a huge town shining in the distance.

'There,' said Laloo, 'you will find fortune. And now, farewell!' And he turned and sprang back into the forest.

Left alone, Roshun went towards the town before him. When he reached its gates a town-crier emerged from them, beating his drum and reading his proclamation. The Prince hurried forward to hear what he was saying.

'Be it known,' cried the man, 'that the king will appoint as his heir the man who can rid this country of the flying-foxes that destroy the crops and fruit, and can slay the serpent that lies on the river bank and devours all who go to bathe!'

'Take me to the King,' said Roshun. 'I will undertake to perform both these tasks.'

He was led to the palace, and there the king received him kindly, and said he should begin

his task next day, but this day must be given up to feasting.

Roshun was entertained by conjurors, musicians, dancers and wrestlers, and at last went to his room for the night. When all sounds in the palace had died down, he opened his window, and gave the call he used to summon his monkey.

In a few minutes he saw small black forms springing up towards his room, and presently the room was full of monkeys, while a great crowd of them remained outside. Roshun hurriedly told the monkeys of the task he had undertaken. One of the older animals said:

'We will rid the King of the flying-foxes tonight, but the serpent will be a more difficult matter. You must do battle with him, but remember to call on us when he is too strong for you.'

The monkeys then left the room as silently as they had come, and the Prince went to bed.

He was woken in the morning by excited voices in the courtyard, and dressed and went down to the King's audience chamber. The King was seated there in state, and as Roshun approached he signalled to a slave, who went up to him and flung a chain of glittering rubies round the Prince's neck.

'You have succeeded splendidly in your first task,' said the King. 'We found thousands of foxes neatly piled together in the gardens. You have now to face the wicked serpent, and then I shall proclaim the fact that you are my heir!'

A beautiful sword was given to Prince Roshun, and he was conducted to the river bank. There he was left, the slaves telling him that the serpent would appear as soon as it found Roshun was alone. The Prince stood upright, his heart beating quickly.

A deep hiss made him turn, and he saw a huge black snake writhing along the ground towards him. He attacked the creature with his sword, and a fierce battle began.

The snake managed to get its coils round the Prince's body, and he felt himself being squeezed dreadfully. He faintly gave Laloo's call, and, to his joy, it was immediately answered by hundreds of monkeys, armed with the huge dagger-like thorns of the wild plum-tree.

They attacked the serpent, stabbing it in hundreds of places until it writhed in agony. Its coils loosened, and Roshun was able to chop off its head with one blow.

The Prince then fell fainting to the earth, while the monkeys chattered and sprinkled his face with water from the river.

When the King's slaves appeared they found the Prince standing by the coils of the dead snake, a troop of monkeys surrounding them. The Prince insisted on the monkeys returning to the palace with him.

There he told the King how they had helped him, and as a reward they were allowed to carry back to the forest with them as much fruit and sweet-stuff as they required.

The Prince was then dressed in splendid robes, and was hailed as the King's heir by everyone.

Now the King decided to find a worthy bride for Prince Roshun, but when he mentioned this to the Prince the latter remembered his lotus-bud, and went in search of it. He found it, still fresh, in the pocket of his old coat, and brought it down to the King. He placed it at the foot of the throne, and told his story to the King, who listened attentively. When he had finished he glanced at the bud, and, to his amazement, saw that it was expanding.

It grew till it was a yard across, and then its petals opened gently, and out stepped a radiantly beautiful Princess, dressed in a gown of tissue woven with gold and silver, and wearing a light veil, sewn with diamond drops, over her face.

The King summoned his Court, and the Prince and Princess were married with great pomp and lived happily at the palace, where Roshun later ruled as king, and received his elder brothers and their wives.

# Jacolino, the farmer's boy

JACOLINO, the farmer's son, was a bright schoolboy, with many friends. Not far from the school-house was the sea, and after school hours the children often went down to the shore to play and fish.

They did some funny fishing! One day a boy fished out a pretty living kitten – a Blue Persian with the loveliest fur.

'Give it to me,' begged Jacolino.

'No,' said the other boy, 'I can't give it to you. It is such a darling little cat, and you don't have the money to pay for it.'

'I *have*!' exclaimed Jacolino. 'See! Here are two silver sixpences.'

Then the boy took the money and gave the cat to Jacolino. When he took her home his father and mother were pleased, and gave him three sixpences as a reward.

The next day, when the boys were fishing, one of them pulled out a fine, handsome dog. 'This is worth more than the cat,' said the boy. 'Who will buy him for three silver sixpences?'

'I will!' cried Jacolino, bringing the money out of his pocket.

The dog was handed over to him, and he took it home. His parents were very pleased.

'This dog will catch the rats,' they said. And they gave Jacolino four silver sixpences as a reward for bringing home the dog.

On the third day some of the children fished out of the sea a beautifully marked little snake.

Greedy Jacolino wanted this also, and bought it from the others with his four silver sixpences. This time, however, his father and mother were not at all pleased, and they scolded him for bringing such a 'horrid creature' into the house.

'Very well,' said Jacolino, 'as you do not like my pretty snake, I will take him away.'

He put the snake into his breast-pocket and walked off to the town. As Jacolino passed the King's palace the Princess saw him from her window.

'Look, father!' she said to the King. 'See what a handsome boy is passing. *Do* take him into our service!'

The King, who always did as his daughter asked, immediately called in the boy and asked him what kind of work he would like to do.

Jacolino, who was not at all particular, said that he would be glad to do anything.

He was taken on as an under-gardener, and he worked so cleverly and behaved so well that he won the good opinion of all who knew him.

He still kept the snake hidden in his breast-pocket, taking it out at night, and now and then during the day when no one was about.

One day the snake spoke to Jacolino for the first time.

'You work much too hard here, dear master,' he said. 'Go to the King, thank him for his kindness, and then let us leave this place.'

At first Jacolino refused to do this, for he

loved the good King and his charming daughter, and did not want to leave them. But the snake would not let him rest, and so at last he gave in, and asked the King's permission to take a holiday.

'Take one by all means,' said the King. 'You well deserve it. But be sure you come back to us, for we can't spare you altogether.'

Jacolino promised to return. Then he and his pet set off on their travels.

'My dear master and friend,' said the snake, wriggling out of Jacolino's pocket when they had left palace and town far behind, 'for a long time you have kindly taken care of me, now you must let me do something for you. Sit down on my back.'

Jacolino did as he was told, and the snake swelled out until he was immensely big and strong, and the boy's feet did not touch the ground. The snake then made his way into a little wood, where he stopped in front of a hollow tree. From this tree he took a whistle, which he gave to Jacolino.

The boy was very glad to get off his friend's back, for the wriggling had made him feel giddy and seasick. He looked doubtfully at the whistle.

'What am I to do with this?' he asked.

'Blow it,' said the snake, 'and my father will appear. He is a dragon, with twelve heads, but don't be afraid of him. Ask him for the ring which he wears on his finger.'

Presently he saw the dragon coming towards them. Jacolino was not in the least frightened.

'Well,' said this monster to his son, 'where have you been all this long time?'

'An eagle flew away with me and dropped me into the sea,' replied the snake. 'Some children who were fishing drew me out, then this kind friend bought me for four silver sixpences.

'Oh, indeed?' said the dragon carelessly. He looked at Jacolino. 'What,' he inquired, 'do you ask in return for your care of my son?'

'Nothing but that gold ring which I see on your finger.'

'You can't have *that*!' said the dragon snappishly. 'Ask me for something else.'

'No, no, *no*!' cried the snake. 'Give him the ring, father. He *shall* have the ring!'

'He shall *not* have the ring!' roared the dragon.

The snake and the dragon began to fight. Both were very strong, but the snake – though he did not look it – was the stronger, and the dragon had to give up the gold ring.

'Put this on your finger,' said the snake to Jacolino. 'Whenever you are in need of anything turn the ring three times, then three giants will jump out of it and hasten to obey your commands. If you use these servants of yours wisely you will very soon be the richest man on earth. Now, I am sorry to say, I must stay here with my father, but I shall never forget you, and I hope that you will not quite forget *me*.'

'Never!' said the boy. He felt very sad at having to part with his friend the snake, but as he walked on towards his home he cheered up and, though he was not particularly in need of anything, he thought that he would just turn the ring and see what would happen. He turned it three times, and immediately the three giants jumped out.

'What does our master require?' they asked eagerly, all speaking together.

'I want two of you to go on before me, and turn my father's house into a splendid castle. I want the other one to stay with me and carry me home.'

Jacolino's orders were instantly obeyed. Two of the giants went on, the other carried him home. There Jacolino found his father and mother sitting in a grand castle without knowing in the least how they got there. The cat and dog were lying on a magnificent rug in front of the fire.

Jacolino related his adventures, and told his parents that the dearest wish of his heart was to

W
HEATH
ROBINSON

marry the beautiful Princess. The very next
day Jacolino's mother went to see the King, to
whom she said that her son, the former
gardener-boy, having become a great and
powerful person, desired to marry His
Majesty's daughter.

'Well,' said the King, 'he may have her if he
can do two things.'

'What are they?' asked the woman.

'We will take one at a time,' replied the
King. 'The first thing is this – that between my
palace and your castle twelve regiments of
soldiers shall be posted tonight, with all their
bands playing, one as beautifully as another.'

The mother went home and told Jacolino
what the King had said.

'All right,' said the young man cheerfully.
'I'll soon do that!'

At midnight he went outside the castle and
turned his ring three times.

The three giants appeared.

'What are your orders, master?' they
inquired.

'That tonight between my castle and the
King's palace shall be posted twelve regiments
of soldiers, with all their bands playing, one as
beautifully as another.'

'It shall be done, master,' they said.

Very early in the morning the King was
awakened by the sound of music. As soon as it
was light he looked from his window and saw
the twelve regiments of soldiers drawn up
below. All their bands were playing in perfect
tune and time.

'Wonderful!' exclaimed the King.

After this he sent to tell Jacolino the second

thing which he had to do before he could marry the Princess.

This was the message:

'Near my palace there is a very bare mountain. By tomorrow turn it into a vineyard, and arrange that two quarts of wine from it shall stand on my breakfast table.'

Of course, the three giants easily managed this.

Then Jacolino was allowed to marry the beautiful Princess, who loved him every bit as much as he loved her.

Soon after the wedding the old King died, and the lady became Queen Jacolino. Her husband, King Jacolino, often lent her his magic ring.

One day she gave him a pleasant surprise, by sending the giants to fetch his old friend the snake.

As the dragon was now dead the snake was easily persuaded to make the palace his home.

'Had it not been for you,' Jacolino said to the snake, 'I should never have become King and lived in this wonderful palace.'

'And had it not been for you,' replied the grateful snake, 'I might have been thrown back into the sea again. It is to you that I owe everything.'

So the snake now keeps guard over the entrance to Jacolino's home.

And a very happy home it is, too.

# The magic harp

Once upon a time in the East there lived a poor boy named Selim, whose father was so poor when he died that he left nothing but debts behind him.

When he was buried his creditors came and turned poor Selim out of the house.

'All these goods belong to us,' they said to him.

Now, poor Selim was very fond of his father and he begged to be allowed to take away some little thing to remember him by. But the creditors refused.

'You must take nothing of more value than the things to be found on the dust-heap,' they said.

So poor Selim went and looked on the dust-heap, and there he found an old staff and the remains of an old harp, which he remembered his father had bought out of charity from a poor stranger, even poorer than himself.

'Can I take these?' said Selim.

So the creditors laughed when he showed them the two things he had picked up from the dust-heap.

'Yes, you can take them,' they said.

Then they turned Selim from the door, and away he went into the wide world to look for his bread, with nothing but the staff and the old harp to bear him company. Selim felt very sad, for he had not a friend in the wide world, and he did not know where to go.

He wandered on for a long time through a desert country, and presently, when it got towards evening, he began to believe he was lost.

Luckily there were some fruit trees about, and he managed to gather enough to satisfy his hunger.

When the moon rose he hung the old harp on the bough of a tree above him, and lay down to rest with the staff beside him.

He was just closing his eyes to sleep when the wind stirred in the leaves above him, and the old harp began to sing.

'Selim! Selim! Keep a brave heart!' it sang. 'Keep a brave heart, and soon fortune will be yours!'

Selim opened his eyes and sprang to his feet.

'Who speaks?' he cried.

'I speak,' said the harp. 'I am the harp of the man to whom your father gave his last coin. I will never deceive you, Selim, and if you follow my instructions you will soon find a treasure that will make you rich for life.'

'What am I to do, then?' asked Selim, who could not decide whether he was asleep or dreaming.

'In the rocky hills ahead of you there is a cave,' sighed the wind in the harp strings. 'In the cave an enchanted princess lies sleeping.

'She is more beautiful than the moon or the stars, and it is written that she will marry the man who succeeds in awakening her.

'I will show you the way.'

'Let me set forth at once, then!' cried Selim. So he seized the harp and the staff, and he set out once more on his travels.

The farther he went the wilder and stranger grew the way. He had surely reached an enchanted country where everything was sunk in magic slumber.

But the moon was full, and though the way was very long Selim's heart did not fail him, for whenever he felt tired or his courage failed, the wind in the strings of the old harp sang to him:

'Courage, Selim, courage! You have not very far to go now.'

Presently Selim came to the foot of a rocky mountain, and in the mountain he saw the entrance to a great cave.

'And here the wind blew strongly in the harp and a joyful sound came from it, so that Selim's heart rose high, feeling that he had come to the close of his wonderful journey.

He was just about to lay aside the harp and enter the cave, when there was suddenly a savage roar, and a great lion sprang out from the entrance to the cave, snarling and lashing his tail.

'Harp, harp, you have deceived me!' cried Selim. And he shrank away from the entrance of the cave, fearing every moment that the lion would spring upon him and devour him.

'No, no, I have not deceived you!' said the harp. 'Fear nothing, for you have another friend at hand to help you.'

'And who is that?' cried Selim.

'It is I!' cried the staff he carried in his hand. 'For I am the staff belonging to the man to whom your father gave his last coin, and nothing in the world will hurt you while I am here.'

With that the staff sprang from his hand, and at once attacked the lion, and, though the lion snarled and bounded into the air, trying to get hold of it, the staff was much too quick for him.

Thump! Thwack! went the stick on the lion's sides, and gave him such a severe thrashing that he fled, howling, away into the desert.

'Any more enemies to be faced?' said Selim to the staff.

'There may be or there may not be,' said the staff boldly. 'But if there are, I will face them for you.'

With that the staff entered the cave first, and Selim followed, with the wind laughing softly through the strings of the harp.

No sooner had he entered than a dragon raised its head.

Bang! Thwack! went the staff, and it seemed the dragon had even less heart than the lion, for, after a blow or two, he uttered a cry and went flying out into the desert.

Then Selim looked about him, and he saw the cave was full of a rosy glow.

The glow came from innumerable jewels which studded the walls of the cave. And on a couch an enchanted princess was lying.

Selim stole forward and took her hand, and at once the harp uttered a great twang, the strings snapped, and the enchanted princess woke up.

Selim led her to her home, a beautiful palace not very far away, where they were married soon after to the great rejoicing of her subjects.

But, strange to say, the magic harp and the wonderful staff never spoke again.

# The hat full of soldiers

A POOR cobbler once lived in a small village. He mended shoes so well for his neighbours that there was very little work they could give him to do. So he grew poorer and poorer, until at last there came a day when there was nothing more in the house to eat, and his only possession was an old she-goat. The cobbler then decided that he must go and seek his fortune elsewhere.

'You see how it is,' he said to his old wife, 'it is impossible for me to stay here any longer, for there is no more work for me to do, and soon we shall starve. I must therefore kill the old she-goat, so that you may cook me some meat to carry with me on the journey.'

The goat was killed the next day. The cobbler took a piece of the flesh, and, leaving the rest for his wife, set out along the road. He journeyed all day, but came neither to town nor village, nor any inhabited spot. At last, when night was closing in, he reached a place where an old statue stood by the roadside. He lay down beside this to rest, and was beginning to eat a little meat, when suddenly the statue above him spoke.

'What have you in that bundle?' asked the statue.

'I have nothing but a little goat's flesh,' replied the astonished cobbler, 'for I am a poor man, and travel in search of my fortune.'

'Do not eat the goat's flesh,' said the statue, 'but take it with you to the bend of the road. There you will see a small wooden hut, in which a band of imps have their workshop. Throw the goat's flesh inside the hut; and when the imps ask what payment you require, demand from them the old rag which lies on the bed. Refuse all other payment, and it will be well with you.'

Obedient to these instructions, the cobbler got up and walked to the bend of the road, where he found, as the statue had foretold, a small wooden hut. Walking up to the door, he threw in his meat. At once he heard the voices of the imps asking what payment he wanted.

'The old rag which lies on the bed,' said the cobbler.

The imps cried out that it was impossible, but the cobbler stuck to his point, and in the end the rag was handed out to him.

The cobbler took it and returned to the statue. On the way he examined the supposed treasure, and found it a miserable thing, far worse than any which he had left behind in his own house. He complained bitterly to the statue, which he considered had tricked him by such poor advice.

'Do not be so hasty,' said the statue. 'Take the rod which you see in my hand, and, having placed the rag flat on the ground, tap three times upon it.'

The cobbler did as he was bid, and immediately the rag was covered with a wonder-

ful spread of appetising dishes! The hungry cobbler fell to with a will, for it was long since he had tasted such excellent food; and he saw plainly that thanks to the statue he had a magic rag which would keep him from need.

Having finished his meal, the cobbler rolled up the rag, gave grateful thanks to the statue, and took the road for home. But it was late when he started, and he was obliged to pass the night at an inn. While there he could not resist showing everyone present the magical properties of his precious rag. All were much astonished. The host and his wife decided that they must have the rag, and determined that when the cobbler was asleep they would steal it. During the night, therefore, the host took it from the cobbler's bedside, leaving in its place another which looked just like it.

Morning came, and the cobbler paid his bill and left. When he reached home he invited all his friends to share a feast with him. His neighbours gathered, but were surprised to find the table bare. Then the cobbler produced the rag which he had brought home, and, placing it on the table, related the marvellous adventure of the previous day.

When his story was finished, the cobbler struck three times on the rag with the rod which he had taken from the statue's hand. But no dishes appeared, and the company waited expectantly. Puzzled, the cobbler again struck three times, with no better result. Repeated efforts proved equally useless, and the cobbler, whose house was as empty as when he left it, was obliged to send his neighbours away hungry.

The unfortunate man attributed his bad luck to the statue, and determined to take his complaint to it. He therefore took another piece of meat, and went back to the spot where he had rested. But, in reply to his complaints, the statue told him to take the second piece of meat to the imps' workshop and throw it in as before, and this time ask them for the old hat that hung behind the door.

In this way the cobbler was given the hat, and brought it to his mysterious benefactor. The statue produced a second rod, and told the cobbler to tap with it on the hat, after placing the latter on the ground. This was no sooner done than a regiment of soldiers marched out of the hat, formed up and waited for orders.

The cobbler looked with delight at his miniature army, and made it perform various

W. HEATH ROBINSON.

manoeuvres. Then he struck the hat once more, and the soldiers marched into it and disappeared. The cobbler was delighted, for the statue explained to him that on the previous occasion he had been tricked by the dishonest innkeeper, and here was a way in which revenge could be obtained. Away he went to the inn, taking the shabby old hat with him. Confronting the host, he demanded the return of his rag, but the innkeeper denied that he had stolen it. At once the cobbler tapped on the hat,

and in an instant the soldiers filled the taproom, and took the innkeeper prisoner, threatening him with death if he did not return the stolen goods. The terrified man at once gave them up, and the cobbler went on his way, a rich man.

Before he reached home, however, the cobbler sent a message to the king, inviting him to come and witness the strange things which he promised he could show him. The king duly arrived, and the cobbler revealed to him the magic properties of the rag. The king was delighted, and, being no more honest than the innkeeper, ordered his servants to seize the cobbler's goods. In vain did the cobbler protest – the king merely laughed, and told him to think himself lucky not to be thrown into prison. The cobbler then stood upon his dignity, and declared war on the king. The latter

was much amused at the challenge, but appointed a day, in one month's time, when the issue should be decided.

In due course the important day arrived. The cobbler, equipped only with the magic hat, appeared on the chosen field of battle. The king came with a squad of ten picked soldiers, and was delighted when he found his opponent without a force of any kind. He laughed too soon, however, for the cobbler placed his hat on the ground, and beat on it three times with the rod. Out marched the famous regiment of soldiers, which promptly surrounded the king's bodyguard and took the monarch himself prisoner. The king was obliged t urrender, but was released on giving a promise to restore the stolen goods.

The cobbler returned to his home, and lived happily and prosperously with the precious rag, which none dared to try to steal, for fear of the soldiers hidden in the old hat!

# Stupider and stupider

A s HE went off to the fields one morning, a farm-hand reminded his wife that she must not forget to send his dinner to him at midday. Having prepared the meal the wife told her daughter to carry it to her father. The girl set out along the road. She covered half the distance, and then stopped at the edge of a big field, where she sat down to rest in the shade of a tree, and began to daydream.

'Without doubt,' she said to herself, 'I shall marry before long, and perhaps I shall have a son. I shall call him John. But supposing he should die—'

Without more ado she burst into tears.

'Alas, my dear, sweet little John!'

Her tears fell faster and faster, and her grief was so intense that she did not notice how the time went by. As she did not return, the mother eventually went in search of her daughter, and found her crying at the foot of a tree. The young girl explained the reason for her grief.

'It makes me weep to think,' she said, 'that I may have a son, and may lose him.'

At these words the woman, too, burst into sobs.

'Poor grandmother,' she cried, 'poor mother, poor little child! What a sad fate!'

They stayed together inconsolable until evening came, quite forgetting the father's meal.

When night fell, however, the father returned home extremely annoyed at not having had his dinner. He found his wife and daughter in tears, with their arms around each other.

'What is all this?' he demanded. 'Why did you bring me nothing to eat? What are you both crying for?'

His wife told him the reason for their great sorrow.

'Oh, what idiots!' he cried angrily. 'There cannot be in all the world two such geese as you!' And he left the house and made his way to a neighbouring village.

In this place there were some people building a house, and as one of the beams was too short several of them were tugging at each end with all their strength, in order to make it longer. Of course, their efforts were useless.

'What are you doing there?' asked the workman, very much interested.

They explained matters to him.

'What will you give me if I show you how to lengthen the beam?'

'Anything you like, but we do not think your efforts will succeed any better than our own.'

The workman took a second beam and nailed it firmly to the first one to make it double the length. The villagers were astonished, and gave him a large sum of money with many compliments.

A little farther on he went through a hamlet

where some masons had just finished putting up a house without windows. Their plan for getting light into it was to collect some sunbeams in a box and carry it into the house.

'What extraordinary job are you busy with?' asked the workman.

'We want to find a means of letting light into this house, but we see very plainly that the thing is impossible, and therefore we must give it up.'

The workman had no difficulty in cutting a window in the wall, and the sunlight instantly shone in. The masons were greatly impressed, and begged him to accept several gold coins.

In a third village he saw a man who was puzzled as to how to put on a pair of trousers which he had just bought. The fellow had climbed a tree, and was getting ready to jump into the legs of the trousers. The workman showed him the ordinary way of putting on a pair of trousers, and again received a handsome present for his advice.

Farther on he found an old woman who had gone into her neighbour's house in order to ask for a handful of salt. She had found no difficulty in putting her hand into the salt box, but when she had taken hold of the salt she could not get it out again, as her fist was tightly clenched. Everybody in the village, including the doctor, was gathered round her, discussing the case of this poor woman pinned by her arm. The workman went up to the woman and struck

her sharply on the wrist with his stick. The pain made her let go the salt. She opened her fist, and pulled out her hand without difficulty.

The astonished villagers were almost inclined to look on this as a miracle. They made a collection, and handed over the proceeds to the clever workman.

Still going on his way, the workman met two young women who were washing linen, with a little sucking-pig running about near them. He decided to test once again the stupidity of the people of this neighbourhood.

'Good day,' he said: 'Heaven protect you!'

'Thank you. The same to you.'

'Do you know, my pretty maids, why I am here?'

'No. What do you want?'

'Why, the brother of this little pig is being married today, and I have come to fetch him, so that he may be a page of honour.'

At once the two women were in a flutter, running about and getting very busy over the animal.

'Quick,' said one, 'get your satin kerchief for him!'

'Here, buckle this belt upon him!'

'Wait, here is my coral necklace and pretty silk petticoat with the green and pink stripes!'

They chattered away without stopping. You ought to have seen the commotion they made, while all the time the little pig grunted!

The workman then took the sucking-pig away. As soon as he had left the village he took the ornaments off, and drove the pig away over the fields.

The two women presently went back to their homes and told their husbands the story of the little pig which had gone to be a page of honour.

The men at once got very angry and cried out to their wives:

'Idiots! Couldn't you see that the fellow was laughing at you, and has stolen the pig? Quick, let's be after the thief!'

One of them jumped quickly on his horse and overtook the workman.

'Say, friend, have you happened to pass a peasant leading a sucking-pig on a string?' he asked.

'Why, yes, only a moment ago. He has just taken a path across these fields. If you want to catch him up, run after him quickly. I will look after your horse.'

The man (no less stupid, after all, than his wife) got down from his horse and handed the bridle to the workman, who jumped on the horse and returned to his house at a gallop.

'Well,' said he, when he met his wife and daughter again, 'I have found some people even more foolish than you, which is lucky for both, or otherwise I should have given the pair of you a first-rate beating!'

# More Beaver Books

We hope you have enjoyed this Beaver Book. Here are some of the other titles:

**Rhyme Time** A Beaver original. Over 200 poems specially chosen by Barbara Ireson to introduce younger readers to the pleasures of reading verse. This lively collection is illustrated throughout by Lesley Smith

**The Terribly Plain Princess** A collection of original and amusing fairy tales for younger readers, written by Pamela Oldfield and illustrated by Glenys Ambrus

**Carina and the Wild Boy** Carina is the first person to see the wild boy, early one morning in the forest, and they soon become friends. But the grown-ups, in particular King Gilga Mesh, soon realise that Inkydoo could be very useful to them.... Andrew Sinclair's first novel for children is illustrated by Krystyna Turska

**The Adventures of John and Tigger** John, William and Mary Carter know lots of lovely people, and one of them is John's best friend Tigger, the champion bun-eater! Written by Delia Huddy and illustrated by John Spiers for younger readers

**Covens and Cauldrons** An anthology of stories, folk tales, poems and legends about witches, edited by Jacynth Hope-Simpson and strikingly illustrated by Krystyna Turska

**Miss Hickory** The resourceful Miss Hickory, made of a hickory nut and an apple twig, finds she has to adapt to a new life when she is turned out of her corncob house one winter. Written by Carolyn Sherwin Bailey and illustrated by Ruth Gannett, this enchanting story was first published in 1946 and won its author the Newbery Medal. For readers of eight to twelve

These and many other Beavers are available at your local bookshop or newsagent, or can be ordered direct from: Hamlyn Paperback Cash Sales, PO Box 11, Falmouth, Cornwall TR10 9EN. Send a cheque or postal order, made payable to The Hamlyn Publishing Group, for the price of the book plus postage at the following rates:
UK: 22p for the first book plus 10p a copy for each extra book ordered to a maximum of 92p;
BFPO and EIRE: 22p for the first book plus 10p a copy for the next 6 books and thereafter 4p a book;
OVERSEAS: 30p for the first book and 10p for each extra book.

New Beavers are published every month and if you would like the *Beaver Bulletin*, which gives a complete list of books and prices, including new titles, send a large stamped addressed envelope to:

**Beaver Bulletin**
The Hamlyn Group
Astronaut House
Feltham
Middlesex TW14 9AR

200159